EVENTIDE

Also by Therese Bohman

THE OTHER WOMAN
DROWNED

EVENTIDE

THERESE BOHMAN

Translated from the Swedish by Marlaine Delargy

OTHER PRESS
NEW YORK

The translation of this work was supported by a grant from the Swedish Arts Council.

Production editor: Yvonne E. Cárdenas
Text designer: Jennifer Daddio
This book was set in Mrs. Eaves and Adobe Garamond
1 3 5 7 9 10 8 6 4 2

LIBRARY OF CONGRESS CATALOGING-IN-PUBLICATION DATA

Names: Bohman, Therese, 1978– author. | Delargy, Marlaine, translator.
Title: Eventide / Therese Bohman ; translated by Marlaine Delargy.
Other titles: Aftonland. English.
Description: New York : Other Press, 2018.
Identifiers: LCCN 2017032527 (print) | LCCN 2017034674 (ebook) |
ISBN 9781590518946 (ebook) | ISBN 9781590518939 (paperback)
Subjects: LCSH: College teachers—Sweden—Fiction. | BISAC: FICTION / Contemporary Women. | FICTION / Psychological. | FICTION / Literary. | LCGFT: Psychological fiction
Classification: LCC PT9877.12.O48 (ebook) | LCC PT9877.12.O48 A6713 2016 (print) |
DDC 839.73/8—dc23
LC record available at https://lccn.loc.gov/2017032527

Midway in the journey of our life
I found myself in a dark wood,
for the straight way was lost.
—DANTE ALIGHIERI

I think God is German
There is a grace in everything that is organized
—JONATHAN JOHANSSON

EVENTIDE

The subway car was packed and she had to stand from Slussen to Östermalmstorg, crammed between people who all seemed to be sweating. The whole car stank. The trains were still running according to the summer schedule, which meant half as many departures as usual, in spite of the fact that most vacationers were back in the city by now. It was the end of August, the heat still heavy and sticky in Stockholm. It had been an unusually warm summer.

The few people who alighted at the University station formed an orderly line on the long escalator heading up toward the daylight; most of them were suntanned teenagers, possibly there to find their way around before the start of the semester in a few days' time.

They get younger every year, she thought—as she did every August/September. At first glance she wouldn't even have said that some of them were old enough for high school. But now they would be studying at the University of Stockholm, possibly in her own department. She glanced along the path leading toward the blue buildings; it was hard to tell. In their summer clothes, all students looked the same.

The department was everything the subway wasn't: cool and quiet. A printer was chugging away farther down the corridor, and the faint smell of paper and stuffy rooms hovered in the air. She was very happy here in spite of the total lack of glamour, in spite of the fact that the corridors with their flat-woven plastic rugs made the place look like just about any public facility—a community center in a small town, an elementary school, a clinic. The exterior of the ivy-covered brick building was beautiful; it was one of the few impressive structures on the campus. And she loved the nameplate on her door, "Karolina Andersson, Professor of Art," even though she didn't really like her own name. It was a boring name, a typical 1970s name without the slightest hint of mystery, easily forgotten, but at least the title lifted it somewhat. One day she would probably get used to "Professor of Art," but she wasn't there yet.

The air quality in her room was poor, and she randomly turned the air-conditioning dial, or maybe it was the heating; she had never understood how it worked. Then she opened the window instead. She had a view of the Natural History Museum, and she never tired of looking at it. It was a long time since she had been in there—at least ten years, possibly fifteen. Or even twenty. The speed with which time passed often frightened her. The years since she left school and moved away from home felt like a moment compared with her childhood and teens, which seemed to have gone on for an eternity.

When she was working on the weekend she would often gaze out at the procession of families heading from the subway station to the entrance of the museum, full of enthusiasm at the prospect of seeing films about the universe or the Antarctic, skeletons of whales, models of dinosaurs, stuffed animals. Actually, it was probably more like twenty-five years since she had been in there. She really ought to go. Tomorrow, perhaps. The rooms were bound to be pleasantly cool.

She spent a few hours going through her mail and checking her messages, which mostly consisted of information about various activities, guest lectures, invitations to apply for research funding. Luncheon vouchers for the Faculty Club, where she never ate. The agenda for the first board meeting of the new semester. And a message from one of her PhD students, sloppily written and sent late the previous night.

She stretched and stood up to go and get a coffee. An indolent atmosphere pervaded the entire building, a late summer drowsiness, which within days would be supplanted by activity and stress. She loved being here when the department was deserted. She had spent most of the Easter break at her desk, absorbed in her work. It was a good memory.

Peter Tallfalk was in the staff room waiting for the machine to finish producing a cup of coffee. Peter was also a professor, and Tallfalk was a name he had adopted when he got married a few years ago. Karolina thought it was an amusing name, with its pretensions to distinguished elegance even though it made him sound like a character from a children's book. Mr. Tallfalk.

But Peter was nice; of all her colleagues, he was the one she liked best. He was in his sixties and his particular focus was iconology in the successors of Panofsky, which seemed strangely old-fashioned among all the more contemporary research projects currently ongoing within the department. Peter had a rare passion for graphics, primarily from the Renaissance. His appearance was rather mousy, but in a nice way; more rodent than falcon.

He seemed pleased to see her.

"How was your summer?" he asked as Karolina pressed a button on the machine.

"Okay." She hesitated briefly. "I've been busy with the move most of the time."

He nodded sympathetically.

"Of course. All sorted?"

"I wouldn't say that exactly, but I've unpacked everything. And redecorated, so at least there's a kind of superficial order."

She pulled a face while he continued to exude sympathy.

She had moved from a large three-room apartment in Vasastan to a small two-room place in Södermalm. At the same time she had gone from eleven years of living with a partner to life as a singleton, and she knew it was going to take a while to get used to that. She had, however, quickly grown accustomed to the pitying looks that said: "Women in their forties don't dump their partner. You've really made a mess of things now."

"We're late bloomers, you and I," Peter said. "Like all the best people."

She smiled, touched at his kindness.

"You must come over for a drink one evening," he went on. "It's still possible to sit out, and we're planning on doing just that right through the fall. We've installed infrared heating. Well, I say we—I got someone in to do it. I don't have a handy bone in my body."

Karolina thought the apartment still had a slightly strange odor, as if she hadn't yet made her mark. An acrid smell lingered in the rooms; she thought it might be the cheap detergent used by the cleaning company.

Otherwise she was happy here, in a passive kind of way. It was a beautiful apartment, even though it was pretty shabby, and in an area she wouldn't have chosen if she had actually had a choice. Unfortunately the purchase had had to be expedited quickly, and in June, when there wasn't a great deal on the market. She had wanted to move fast. The block was at the end of Folkungagatan, just where it begins to slope down toward the Stadsgård intersection and the Finland ferries, a Södermalm appendix, slightly run-down, with one of the inner city's few remaining petrol stations diagonally opposite. The living room was noisy, with its old windows overlooking the street; they rattled when there was a lot of traffic, and when trucks from the ferries chose to make their way into the city via Folkungagatan.

"Great potential," the property details had said; she knew perfectly well that this could mean almost the same as "in need of significant renovation" in broker-speak. The building had passed into the hands of a tenants' association just a few years earlier. The previous owner was an elderly lady who had since passed away, and she had decided not to go in for the hysterical refurbishment which most people of Karolina's generation had opted for. This apartment bore clear signs of its past; the paint was scuffed on cupboards and door frames, the creaking parquet flooring needed repolishing, and the bathroom floor was covered by a grubby plastic mat that looked as if it had been put down in the eighties, and was long overdue for replacement.

But Karolina liked her new home. It had soon begun to feel like an oasis, a space of her own, maybe somewhere she could make a fresh start, even if that was still some way beyond the horizon. For the moment it was a good location for a period of aimless confusion.

She had repainted the walls during a hot week in July. Every room had been decorated with nondescript, pale wallpaper with a discreet pattern; it didn't particularly bother her, but there were stains here and there that made it look grubby, and it was probably one of the reasons for the comparatively cheap selling price.

She did a fairly slapdash job, sanding down and filling holes in a halfhearted way, wearing only a T-shirt and panties because it was almost thirty degrees Celsius outside, and it was impossible to create a draft indoors. The air in the city was undisturbed for weeks during the summer, hot days and tropical nights. She slapped two coats of Stockholm white on top of her poor preparatory work, then left the windows wide-open all evening while she sat in the little island of furniture in the middle of the living room, drinking chilled white wine and watching the moths attack the expensive candles she had bought in the hope that they would neutralize the smell of paint, which gave her a nagging headache.

"Get yourself a cat," one of her colleagues had said when she moved in, but she refused, even though she actually liked cats. She didn't want to be a single woman with a cat, it was too tragically predictable. "I'd prefer a lover," she had replied, and they had both laughed, even though she was perfectly serious.

Hi Karolina, first of all I'd like to apologize for not keeping in touch. I realize you might have been wondering what I was up to. The thing is, I've found some really interesting material during my stay in Berlin. Ebba Ellis, the subject of my dissertation, turns out to be a far more fascinating person than I could have imagined. I'd really like to discuss the matter with you in more detail now I'm back in Stockholm. I'm so pleased that you're my supervisor! Best, Anton."

It was a cheerful e-mail, but at the same time Karolina couldn't help feeling annoyed. Anton Strömberg had been accepted as a research student a year ago, but she still hadn't met him; all contact had been via e-mail. At first she had thought this was convenient, but then it had begun to seem rather strange, and she had repeatedly asked him to call in at the department. However, he had spent most of his time in Berlin, as he pointed out in every insubstantial message he sent her, as if it were something remarkable. In fact, virtually every Swedish student aiming for a PhD in humanities seemed to spend a considerable amount of time in Berlin.

The carefree tone of this latest e-mail also bothered her. When she was working toward her doctorate she had been constantly full of doubt, both about her topic—Would it be enough? Would it be possible to produce sufficient material, given the limitations she had set in order to avoid the opposite problem: a topic that simply spilled over and became impossible to control—and, above all, doubts about her own capability. Would she succeed in completing the task she had set herself, would she ever finish? With hindsight that period had felt like being trapped inside a bubble, constructed by her own brain and the sad little ideas it managed to come up with, ideas which she hoped she would be able to present in the guise of reliable research. She had constantly felt as if she were trying to con everyone, to bluff her way to a title, as if she would inevitably be exposed, sooner or later. She was woken night after night by bad dreams: she had overslept on the day of her defense, and everything went wrong when she tried to hurry to the university. She had to pack a bag to take with her and couldn't find the things she needed; she realized she had turned up at her own defense without her pants.

Yes, there was definitely an air of self-assurance about this e-mail that irritated her, particularly "I realize you might have been wondering what I was up to." At some point about a year ago she might have wondered in passing what he was actually up to, might have thought that he really ought to come and see her, but after that she had started to think of Anton Strömberg as lost, one of those PhD candidates who would never finish their dissertation, in spite of their talent and potential, because something else got in the way. Life, building a family, illness, the nightlife in Berlin. She simply hadn't bothered about the reason.

It was also annoying that she'd never heard of this Ebba Ellis, who was allegedly so fascinating.

Wikipedia supplied her with brief details. "Swedish artist, born 1864 in Kristianstad, died 1945 in Munich. Ellis studied art in Germany and Paris from 1882. She made her name primarily through her symbolist-influenced graphics."

There was a link to an issue of *Ord & Bild* which contained two illustrations produced by Ellis to accompany a poem by the Finland-Swedish poet Bertel Gripenberg in 1903, "Songs to Salome": lofty, dramatic, erotic. "Others love with the birds' playful twitter," she read, "the love of others is childlike and gentle and good, but Salome's love is poisonous and bitter, for Salome loves with steel and blood."

Ebba Ellis's illustrations depicted a Salome who really did look as if she loved with steel and blood; her expression was intense, and there was something cruel about her half-open mouth that reminded Karolina of a predatory animal. Her long, dark hair cascaded over a body that was both supple and voluptuous, drawn with sensual lines. They were riveting, powerful pictures, clearly the work of someone who had been in very close contact with what was going on in Europe, particularly with regard to German Symbolism. There was something slightly bizarre about them, as in the work of Max Klinger or Otto Greiner, or even Arnold Böcklin.

It was strange that she hadn't seen them before. She had trawled Swedish art history for precisely this kind of image for her doctorate. On the other hand, history was full of dead ends, artists who had never fulfilled their true potential, especially women, for crass reasons such as children and family life. Or because the artist in question was outside the social and professional context of the day, wasn't part of a network, never had any pupils or followers. But the two illustrations in *Ord & Bild* suggested that Ebba Ellis should have had a context. She didn't seem to be a loner whose work had developed beyond the established history of art. She must have been well-traveled, aware, modern.

The sound of muted laughter could be heard from outside. A group of students were sitting on the lawn in the sunshine, eating salad. Karolina should have stopped for lunch long ago, but when she was working she could easily forget both time and space. Sometimes it was late afternoon before she realized she hadn't had anything to eat, or late at night when it occurred to her that she should have gone home hours ago. It used to drive Karl Johan crazy.

She walked over to the blue buildings, six colossal turquoise structures from the late sixties. When she started studying at the University of Stockholm, all her classes had been in there, and she had hated it. How could the location for something so beautiful have such an ugly form, she had wondered, and she still felt exactly the same.

She spent a long time considering the plastic-wrapped sandwiches in the cafeteria, which all looked equally unappetizing. Eventually she took her sandwich and a bottle of mineral water out into the sun and sat down in the shade of a maple tree in a dutiful attempt to make the most of what she suspected was one of the last really lovely summer days. There had been a faint chill in the air for several weeks, even though the days were still warm.

There was a special atmosphere around the campus at the beginning of the semester, a mixture of anxiety and exhilaration. She watched the students as they walked from the subway into the blue buildings. Perhaps this was the first time they had been at a university. Perhaps their lives would be changed by what they learned during the coming weeks, just as her life had been changed during those first months. It was the overwhelming realization of what a university actually was that had made her stay, the amount of knowledge that was gathered there, the fact that it was a place where learning was generated. She had felt homeless until then, like an empty vessel, and everything that was housed in those university buildings breathed life into her: the knowledge, the art, the culture, the tradition. The values she loved with a pathos and a conviction that she knew was old-fashioned, maybe even inappropriate. But if they could do for someone else what they had done for her, then she intended to hold on to them, in the best-case scenario to give them away like a key to someone who needed it, just as she had done, a key that would open up the world, make it seem clear and manageable when all its contexts and connections made sense.

During that very first term she had also come to understand that not everyone shared her conviction—far from it. She remembered a course that was pervaded by the relativism that was fashionable at the time, her shock that both her tutors and the course literature talked of the equal value of all expressions of culture, how she had instinctively known that she didn't think that way. She was aware that the crocheted pot holders and TV soaps held up as examples were simply not as good as the best novels she had read, the best paintings she had seen, or the best architecture she hadn't actually seen in most cases, but could vividly imagine after studying hundreds of pictures: the Acropolis, the Colosseum, Notre Dame. These names seemed to her to possess a sparkling, magical quality; they made her think of the old wireless in her grandparents' summer cottage when she was little. It was the size of a cupboard, and had the most fantastic place names on the panel that glowed softly on those summer evenings: *Luxembourg, Frankfurt, Brussels, Monte Carlo.* Words as beautiful as poetry, shimmering and full of promise like jewels in a casket, words that made her long desperately to be the kind of person who would one day travel to places with names that sounded as magical as Monte Carlo.

This feeling was with her as she contemplated the crocheted pot holders that her university course tried to "sell" her as an insidious plan to get her to accept something paltry, before she had even been given the chance to see the magnificence against which this was a reaction. And she still felt that way. She sometimes had a childish urge to scream "Why do you want to destroy everything?" during the countless faculty meetings where the chronology of the syllabus was once again under consideration, only to be scrapped several meetings down the line in favor of a thematic approach, even for the foundation courses. In her eyes this was a betrayal of all those who had come to the university because of their love of art, seeking a context. All theory is gray, she often thought, like Mephistopheles in *Faust*. Only the golden tree of life springs evergreen.

Back in the department she passed Professor Lennart Olsson's room. Their specialist areas bordered on each other in terms of time; he was interested in the lesser-known Swedish modernists, particularly the women. Karolina had problems with many aspects of Lennart Olsson, apart from the fact that he had been one of the main advocates for the abolition of a chronological approach. She had no time for his combination of superciliousness and opportunism, or his insufferable cockiness over his links to the cultural pages of *Dagens Nyheter*. The previous year he had given a series of lectures on his female modernists at the Museum of Modern Art, which had proved extremely popular. It was held on Friday evenings and was part of the museum's concept of exhibitions, bars and DJs, which brought the inner city's young, conscious consumers of culture out to Skeppsholmen. These lectures had then been published as a book, which had been very favorably received by the critics, and had achieved unusually high sales figures for essays in a relatively unknown field. "A new canon," the headline above the fawning guest review in *DN* had trumpeted. The whole thing had bestowed upon Lennart an aura that was unusual in the department: celebrity status and the respect of people who didn't know much about art, but who worked in adjoining creative industries such as fashion, advertising and PR, along with an entire generation of young feminists.

Lennart had begun to walk a little taller down the corridors after his successes, but to be honest everything about him was seriously boring. In spite of this, Karolina had heard from several sources that he was something of a ladies' man, which made no sense to her at all. In her eyes he was an unremarkable man in his fifties, with ill-fitting clothes and an overinflated opinion of himself.

His door was open, so she popped her head in.

"Lennart?"

He was absorbed in something on his computer screen; he looked as if he were half-asleep. Perhaps he had been to a party the night before.

"Can I ask you something?"

He beckoned her in, nodding graciously.

"Are you familiar with Ebba Ellis?"

"Ebba who?"

"Ebba Ellis. She was active around the turn of the last century, worked mostly in graphics, and appears to have spent a lot of time in Germany. She didn't die until the 1940s, so I thought you might have come across her."

He shook his head. "Never heard of her." He looked totally uninterested.

"I'm supervising a PhD student who is focusing on her, but there seems to be very little written about her."

"Karolina," Lennart intoned in his authoritative, unconsciously patriarchal manner, "the history of art is a compost heap, particularly when it comes to women. The only thing we can do is start digging. Sometimes we find something valuable, but unfortunately the rest of the time there's nothing but dung."

He looked at her as if he had said something incredibly significant. She nodded.

"Okay, Lennart. I'll bear that in mind."

She had only just sat down in her own office when there was a theatrical knock on the door. A young man looked in; he was wearing a shirt in a dull beige that made it look like some kind of uniform, and for a moment she thought he was a courier delivering a book she had forgotten she'd ordered. Then she realized that this was Anton Strömberg, the PhD student she had never met. He looked carefree and totally confident, exactly like a person who writes carefree, confident e-mails. He moved as if this were his room, in spite of the fact that he had taken no more than a couple of steps through the door. He smiled at her.

"Hi, Karolina—Anton Strömberg."

She stood up to shake hands. He was very good-looking: tall, and with a careless ease about his body that was a little provocative.

"I just thought I'd call in and say hi while I'm around," he went on. "Did you get my message?"

"I did, yes. Yes."

"You didn't reply."

His tone was friendly, but with an underlying challenge.

"I was just about to."

That was a lie, and for some reason she thought he could tell.

"So what do you think? About Ebba Ellis?"

"She seems very interesting. I must confess that I'd hardly heard of her until now, but provided you can find enough material to work from, I'm sure it will be fine."

"I've got fantastic material."

"Really? Tell me more."

"For a start," he said, sitting down on the visitor's chair without waiting for an invitation, "hardly anyone has written about Ebba Ellis. In modern times there's nothing at all; she seems to have been completely forgotten."

"There are plenty of artists in that position; in most cases it's because they weren't very good."

She made the comment to test him, even though the pictures she had found on the Internet had piqued her curiosity.

"Or because they produced very little," she added.

"Ebba Ellis produced a great deal," he said. "And it's good. Most of her work is owned by a relative of hers in Skåne. I came across him a few years ago when I was working for an auction house in Malmö; that's how it began. He contacted me to ask for a valuation of Ebba's drawings and graphics. She seems to have been a pretty cool person—very modern and independent. She left Sweden against the will of her family in order to study and hang out in Munich. They wanted her to come home and get married. She also used quite a few erotic motifs, and they didn't like that either. They thought she had embraced a decadent lifestyle down there in Germany. Which she had."

He gave a crooked smile.

"Okay," Karolina said. "So you have access to Ebba Ellis's work."

He leaned closer across the desk.

"And then there are the letters."

"Letters?"

"Yes, they're amazing. That's why I've been in Berlin. That's where they are."

"Speaking of which, you've been away for a year without letting me see a word that you've written. I assume you have been writing?"

"Absolutely," he said, possibly a little evasively. "But as I said, I've spent a lot of time on the letters. Do you like Stuck? Franz von Stuck?"

The question almost made Karolina laugh, it was so unaffected. As if they were at high school and he was asking her about some new band he was really into.

"Of course I like Stuck," she said.

He nodded delightedly, then got to his feet.

"In that case you're going to love this. I have to go, but it was good to meet you. See you again soon, I hope."

With that he was gone as abruptly as he had arrived, which was also irritating. The visit had been conducted entirely on his terms, even though he was the student and she was the professor. The smell of him lingered in the room, she thought, fresh and green with a hint of something sweet, but perhaps it was her imagination.

She had always loathed Medborgarplatsen without really being able to explain why. The weather often seemed to be worse there than in other squares in the city, although of course that was an entirely unreasonable presumption. It was windy every time she emerged from the subway, life felt miserable in a vague, indefinable way, and the huge, open expanse amplified that feeling like an echo chamber.

But right now the evening sun bathed the place in a warm light that was unusually forgiving, people crowded the sidewalk cafés as if they were still on holiday, shiny noses behind raised glasses, great waves of laughter rolling across the square. She turned into Folkungagatan. An eco-bar had opened next door to the ICA supermarket where she preferred to shop; it was packed even though it was still early afternoon.

Before she settled on the art of the last century, she had thought her academic career would focus on the Renaissance. She was particularly fascinated by Mannerism, the final phase of the Italian Renaissance. The epoch that had started out as clear and dewy-fresh as a spring morning, pure and harmonious, became more and more savage and twisted toward the end; the bodies in Mannerist paintings were distorted and elongated, the colors florid and overblown.

She liked the idea of the origin, flowering and fall of artistic periods; there was something comforting about the cyclical nature of it all. Something else will always follow, something that will also flourish, even if it does so in a different form. Mannerism was a magnificent and extravagant final effort in an age when there was no longer any point in thinking of restraint or moderation. Like the shocking collapse of a bunch of tulips, the last uninhibited phase before they wither and die, when they become like caricatures of tulips, just as Mannerism became a caricature of Renaissance art.

She had recently visited an exhibition of photographs from China, beautiful images of intensive building projects in remote provinces, the construction of bridges and skyscrapers, high-level technology slicing into a farming culture that had remained static for thousands of years. According to the brochure, the photographs depicted the late capitalist state. She didn't know anything about economics and had never reflected on the term "late capitalism" before, but now she couldn't stop thinking about it. It was so beautiful. She could see it in her mind's eye, a twilight land of late capitalism: the decadence that precedes a collapse, a permanent dusk where the absurd proportions that contemporary society has assumed cast longer and longer shadows. It reminded her of an article she had read some years ago, about a car factory in Dresden, a spectacular place where the final assembly of Volkswagen's luxury model, the Phaeton, is carried out. Apparently the factory's facades are made entirely of glass; it looks like a cathedral. Anyone who buys a Phaeton is invited to this glass construction to see their car being put together. This process is carried out efficiently and in silence by good-looking engineers in white coats and gloves; everything is dust-free and aesthetically appealing. Then the client drives his newly completed Phaeton out of the factory, across floors made of Canadian maple. She always pictured twilight in Dresden when she thought about it: those glass walls gleaming like jewels in the last rays of the evening sun as capitalism shamelessly exposed itself in an almost pornographic way before the audience inside, a peep show dedicated to luxury consumerism.

Perhaps something else is going on apart from late capitalism, she often thought; perhaps it's the Mannerist phase of capitalism, and perhaps it applies to other things too. Opening a morning newspaper or watching the news on TV made her believe with increasing frequency that most ideologies seemed to be in their Mannerist phase. She could see it on the front pages and in the culture section of both the left and the right: a convulsive, screaming hysteria, possibly a consequence of the feeling of losing ground to the populist criticism of immigration, and on the opposing side the identity politics, the main representatives of which have quickly installed themselves in permanent posts in the world of culture and media and stopped being young and angry, but whose ideas have filtered down and become common currency for every local newspaper reporter, cultural politician and high school principal who wants to appear both enlightened and critically aware.

The bar next to the ICA store was a showground for the Mannerism of the hipster culture. It was frequented by a well-to-do inner-city clientele who had deliberately adopted a series of consumer habits, but who were really just looking for a different way to spend their money. They were an updated version of the yuppies of the 1980s, whom they would probably have condemned as vulgar, but the driving forces behind them were the same: status and consumption. The only difference was that these days eco-friendly wine and locally produced craft beers just happened to be fashionable.

She bought a good brand of chopped tomatoes and a few shallots, then strolled east along Folkungagatan, which quickly became a little seedy in a way that pleased her: small dry cleaners, mysterious shops that promised to fix your cell phone in no time at all, tobacconist after tobacconist, several with hookahs displayed in the window, a handwritten sign that proclaimed "Fax machine available here!"; perhaps it had been in the window, among bars of chocolate that had faded in the sun, since sometime in the nineties.

She spent a long time browsing the shelves in the intensely air-conditioned state-run liquor store just beyond the point where Folkungagatan crossed Tjärhovsgatan. When she was with Karl Johan she had learned to appreciate fine wines, maybe a little more than was good for her. She moved in a world of VIP viewings at auction houses with a plentiful supply of oysters and champagne, exhibitions and networking opportunities, antique fairs, openings and anniversaries, all with an open bar or at least several glasses of wine, often followed by a visit to a club with some of Karl Johan's associates, or maybe even a meal in a restaurant depending on the refreshments that had been served. She had loved it, particularly in the beginning. It had felt glamorous, completely different from her own life as a PhD student.

She often thought that she drank too much. Just a bit too much, but definitely more than the Department of Health, or a doctor, would recommend. Probably quite a lot more. Standing in front of the shelves of French red she tried to imagine the river of wine that passed through her body in a year; it wasn't a pleasant picture. She also drank alone quite often, something that was surrounded by a particular aura of shame and embarrassment; it was frequently held up as a warning sign in articles about an unhealthy approach to the consumption of alcohol. But she enjoyed drinking alone, and as long as you don't feel that you have to drink, it's fine—that was her conclusion. For example, during periods when she spent whole evenings marking exams, it wasn't hard to abstain. And as long as you can get up in the morning without being affected by the wine from the night before, as long as you can do your job and fulfill your obligations and pay your bills, there's no reason to stop.

She reached for a bottle of Burgundy, decided she might as well take two while she was there, then added a box of white. She actually found wine boxes rather vulgar, but there was a special satisfaction in knowing that there was one in the fridge; it was like having her very own horn of plenty.

Back in the apartment she melted a large knob of butter in a pan and added the chopped shallots and a clove of garlic. That was her favorite moment, when the onions almost melted, softened without browning as she kept an eye on them, stirring distractedly. She tipped in the chopped tomatoes, then turned the heat right down and left the sauce to simmer. She had become obsessed by tomato sauce, by using simple, cheap ingredients and taking plenty of time to create something that tasted neither simple nor cheap. When the sauce turned out really well, she experienced something that was the closest to happiness she had felt in a long time.

She ate her tomato sauce with pasta and a glass of wine in front of the computer. She typed "Anton Strömberg" into Google's search box, which resulted in over one hundred thousand hits. Most of them weren't him; they were links to information about a football player from Helsingborg, a real estate agent on the west coast, and a young guy in a band from Linköping, with black kohl around his eyes.

Karolina peered at the screen and couldn't help laughing when she realized that the guy in the band was actually him. She laughed again when she read the caption: *"It was well deserved," says Anton Strömberg, lead singer in the Femmes Fatales after winning the Student Society's music competition Live Link. "We were the best."* The same self-confident smile she had seen across the desk just a few hours earlier.

She glanced at the date of the article: 2009. He looked young, like a boy. A handsome boy.

She spent the next few hours compiling a fragmentary picture of Anton Strömberg. He seemed to have been born and raised in Linköping; he had studied at the university there and had contributed to the Department of Humanities' literary journal: two poems (callow, highly strung), and a review of an exhibition by a young artist she had never heard of. Karolina had also lived and studied in Linköping for a number of years, and therefore immediately felt slightly more drawn to him—or at least as if she could relate to him.

Another link took her to a page where you could upload a list of the books you owned; Anton had an account. She scrolled through his bookshelf: lots of authors from the last century, not just the usual titles by Strindberg and Söderberg that every undergraduate owned. A first edition of Ola Hansson's *Tidens kvinnor*. Baudelaire, some in French. Stefan George, exclusively in German. Bertel Gripenberg's 1903 collection, with the suite of poems to Salome. A long list of art books, catalogues from exhibitions of work from around 1900, both in Sweden and overseas, and a great many books about individual artists, groups and epochs.

They were good books, almost all of them. For a moment she was transported back to when she was twenty, visiting some guy she was interested in, standing there studying his bookshelves. Most collections were predictable to a certain extent, and quite a lot of young men were nowhere near as original as they would have liked to think. Some had a plethora of Sartre, Camus and Dostoevsky; perhaps they were studying philosophy. Others were studying literature and had an extensive range of horror and eroticism, Bataille and the Marquis de Sade. This latter group, she had discovered during the period when she was interested in that particular type, turned out to be surprisingly average in bed, in spite of the voluminous material at their disposal.

She had never come across the kind of young man Anton Strömberg's bookshelf suggested.

She decided to change the listing from alphabetical to chronological order; the last book had been added just under a year ago. Karolina Andersson: *Seduction and Destruction: The Dangerous Woman in Swedish Art at the Turn of the Twentieth Century.*

Of course there was nothing strange about the fact that he had a copy of her dissertation; not many people dealt with her area, particularly in Sweden. Her perception was that the era around the turn of the twentieth century was astonishingly unfashionable within academic circles. She had also noticed that it attracted two types of individual: those who loathed it for ideological reasons, and sought it out in order to destroy it, and those who were drawn to it because of a fascination with the darker sides of life: sex, drugs, decadence, the incurable loneliness of the soul. There was something that united this latter group, she had observed: a kind of fleshiness, an interest in testing the limits, in living life to the fullest. It wasn't a topic for the refined academic with his or her sights set on the Swedish Academy, for example, or a senior post within the art world. There were much safer options in both earlier and later epochs.

However, it did seem curiously fateful that her dissertation was the latest book Anton had posted on the website. She realized she was wondering what he had thought of it.

His e-mail address was given, ant0n.str0mberg, and when she googled it she found a blog in his name, but it hadn't been updated for several years. It appeared to have served as a kind of literary diary; the posts were headed in the same callow, highly strung style as she had seen in his poems. "On the way home I thought for a moment that I met myself"; "Kastanieallee 74, four stories, April twilight outside"; "I like it when you treat me rough, she said."

Her cheeks burned as she read the last post, an account of how the narrator had had sex with a woman who asked him to hit her. He eventually did so, and found that it turned him on.

Perhaps it was no more than a sexual fantasy in literary form, she thought. Just because he wrote about sex didn't necessarily mean that he was particularly interested in it. A guy she had known long ago, one of those with de Sade on his bookshelf, had told her in graphic detail that the most decadent sex you could have was with a goose, cutting its throat in the same moment as you came. Not only would the bird's death throes intensify the orgasm, but you would have simultaneously experienced sodomy, bestiality, necrophilia and sadism. "And gastronomy, because you can eat the goose afterward," he had said with a laugh, presumably hoping to shock her. Then she discovered that he barely even knew what to do with her body in the darkness; she could still remember his inept, cold and sweaty hands on her skin.

However, everything about Anton Strömberg made her think he knew quite a lot about sex, and not just because he had read the right books.

No. She closed the page. Time to pull herself together. In a fit of paranoia she deleted her Internet history, then went in the kitchen and poured the last of the wine down the sink.

Her next research project focused on depictions of animals in art at the turn of the last century. It felt like a logical continuation of everything she had written about women in art, especially all the images of the woman as a vampire, bordering on the animalistic. There was no shortage of examples of the merging of woman and animal, mythological creatures, sphinxes such as those found in the works of Moreau or Khnopff.

And then there were plenty of apes, which had captured her interest. Following the breakthrough of the theory of evolution, the ape acquired a whole new significance in art; Bruegel's painting of two apes from the middle of the sixteenth century was completely different from the apes after Darwin. In Bruegel's work they were still innocent, simply animals, just like any other animal. By the end of the nineteenth century, the ape more than any animal came to represent not only sexuality but the animalistic side of the whole of humanity, the side which was dark, suppressed, and also the aspect of man that was something else, unknown, uncivilized. Yes, she thought, the ape cut through all the relevant questions that could be considered in a university today: gender and class and ethnicity and sexuality; it existed in a terrifying no-man's-land between the classifications of animal and human, nature and culture, civilization and decadence.

She reread Edgar Allan Poe's "The Murders in the Rue Morgue," spent hours late at night googling images of apes in art. She was fascinated by the German painter Gabriel von Max; after studying both anthropology and Darwin's theories, he had acquired an entire family of apes, which he used as models. He often portrayed them in human situations, which made his pictures both bizarre and creepy: apes contemplating a work of art, an ape reading a book. An ape gazing at a skull and considering death—if apes were actually capable of thinking about death, or even had the capacity to understand the concept of death—but that's what it looked like. The most striking sculpture she came across was Emmanuel Frémier's enormous gorilla carrying a naked woman, apparently against her will. It had evoked both horror and admiration at the Paris salon in 1887; today it seemed like the most unfashionable thing imaginable.

An article in the *Daily Mail* caught her attention by chance; a friend of a friend had shared it on Facebook. A male gorilla in a Japanese zoo had achieved almost rock star status since young Japanese women had decided he was incredibly handsome for a gorilla. The article was accompanied by several pictures, and Karolina had to admit that he was pretty stylish—if you could say that about an animal? She made a note in her ideas document, "sexual attraction of the ape?" and scrolled down the page. There was definitely something fascinating about that massive body; it had such weight, such power. In a couple of images he was resting his chin on his hand, looking serious and thoughtful; it was the kind of pose male models adopted when they were advertising designer watches or glasses. "He's essentially the George Clooney of the gorilla world," the article joked, and the comparison wasn't all that far-fetched: the impressive male really did have a kind of remarkable sex appeal.

She rewatched *King Kong* and suddenly decided it was a wonderful film, extremely romantic and genuinely moving. The scene where the gigantic creature was holding the tiny blonde woman in his hand showed real tenderness, she thought. If he wanted to, he could crush her in a second. Wasn't this an image of absolute intimacy, the sense of being utterly at the mercy of another individual, yet at the same time totally safe and secure? Perhaps the huge ape was an incarnation of the sublime, a violent force to which one could subjugate oneself, maybe even a kind of capricious god-figure?

Sometimes she would sit and read for a while in a hotel bar near the central subway station after work. It was always empty, calm and quiet in the early evening when she was there, in sharp contrast to the hustle and bustle of Sergels torg, just a stone's throw away. Occasionally there would be a man on his own having dinner and a couple of beers, presumably on a business trip, and now and again a group of conference delegates would pass through on their way to some kind of activity. Judging by their nervous excitement and the fact they were all dressed up, they were from a small town out in the sticks. The odd overseas tourist turned up, having fallen for the hotel's central location; they clearly didn't realize that the most desolate and inhospitable areas are contained in inner-city Stockholm.

She liked to sit in the bar knowing that she was completely anonymous, drinking a glass of wine as she halfheartedly leafed through her book. She liked to use the beautifully decorated powder room before strolling down to Sergels torg, watching the people scurrying along like ants as they hurried to engagements that were lacking in her life.

When she was younger she had thought that people became more complicated when they were adults, that they started to have more complex thoughts, a more intricate emotional life. But people remained unchanged, driven by mechanisms no more advanced than acknowledgment and appreciation, still worried about how they looked in the eyes of others, still obsessed with the idea of status. The things that conveyed this status had changed, but the striving and the mechanisms were exactly the same as in the schoolyard.

Sometimes she got the feeling they were pretending, that the people she observed in the square were somehow maintaining a series of facades, a distance from life itself. Maybe this was a prerequisite to enable them to live in the way that was expected of an adult, with a family and a career and a varied social life and leisure time spent in a meaningful way, according to all the images peddled by weekend supplements and interior design magazines. It was necessary to fulfill these requirements by chatting to colleagues over lunch about the weekend's activities, and in cheerful, successful status updates on social media. The simple truth was that most other people seemed to have an enviable ability to live their lives without really getting involved too much.

The city center was almost deserted as she set off for home. It was a lovely evening; the air was still warm, the high-rise office buildings in Hötorget towering above her like a 1950s dream of modern city life against the slowly darkening sky. She walked down Hamngatan, through Kungsträdgården and along the quayside at Slussen, where she slunk into McDonald's and bought two cheeseburgers, which she ate as she enjoyed the view from Katarinavägen. It was like a postcard, with Gröna Lund's amusement park sparkling on the other side of the water. The huge ferries that traveled to Finland and back lay at their moorings like grotesque floating blocks.

She didn't love Stockholm, and she probably never would. Every time someone said they loved Stockholm, she assumed they were lying. She regarded the city as a necessity, often an unpleasant one, but she also thought that everything it was accused of was probably true—snootiness, fearfulness, coldness, regimentation. She had never really felt at home here, but she had never really been unhappy either. Much the same could be said of her life as a whole.

She didn't like traveling, so she rarely left the city. Everything associated with travel made her agitated in a way that destroyed most of the pleasure. She hated to plan things a long way in advance because that forced her to think about the future, and the future made her think about death. A trip booked several months ahead always gave rise to the laconic thought "If I'm still alive by then," which left her at best depressed, at worst in a state of severe anxiety.

Once the booking was confirmed, she would start fretting about what could go wrong in the interim period. She worried about falling ill, asking herself with such intensity whether she was getting a cold or flu or the winter vomiting bug that the symptoms would unfailingly appear, making her even more stressed-out. She worried about forgetting things when she was packing, she worried about the airlines' ridiculous restrictions on carrying liquids and how she was going to be able to fit all her beauty products in her hand luggage if she flew without check-ing her bag, and if she did check her bag, she worried about it getting lost. She was afraid of flying, to the extent that she was on the verge of blind panic during every single minute on board the plane; she had to have at least one glass of wine to calm her nerves before takeoff, which made her feel sick if it was early in the morning. She was afraid of vomiting anyway, and it was even worse during a flight; what if she couldn't get to the bathroom in time, what if she wasn't allowed to leave her seat if she felt ill during takeoff or landing? The pressure inside the cabin affected her ears, and she was always half-deaf by the time she got off, slightly tipsy and nauseous, emotionally drained, with a sweaty forehead and a vague sense of gratitude that she was still alive. Once she had retrieved her suitcase from the baggage carousel and was in the hotel room (having worried that the booking hadn't gone through, even though she had e-mailed to request confirmation), she would slowly begin to take pleasure in her trip.

Everyone in Stockholm loved traveling, which supported yet another accusation: everyone had always just come back from Berlin or New York, and seized any opportunity to talk about it. In certain circles she had sometimes created an awkward situation by announcing that she didn't like traveling. Some people almost seemed to take this as a provocation; it was as if she had come straight out and said she was boring and narrow-minded, or even worse: tinged with an aura of nationalism, perhaps a dislike of other cultures, of people in other countries.

That made her think of Anders, in spite of the fact that she had tried not to do so for over a year.

When the National Museum was about to undergo a lengthy renovation project, the friends of the museum had organized a special dinner, a last chance to spend time there before it closed its doors for several years. Right at the top of the magnificent staircase, beautifully laid and decorated long tables had been set out to accommodate the society's board, prominent members—in other words, those who were prepared to donate money—museum staff and various people who were involved in the renovation. Karl Johan had been on the board for a number of years; he was cheerful and relaxed, mingling and chatting and charming both men and women. He had loved getting to know those who were wealthy, and took every opportunity to do so in the hope that it would lead to something. It might be the chance to acquire half a dozen Gustavian chairs at a knock-down price, since they were only cluttering up someone's attic, after all, or a way to burrow into a rich person's life, to be invited to their parties and thus to make even more contacts. One summer he had insisted on taking a vacation in Skåne in order to visit the owners of a castle. He had met them in some context or other and made sure he kept in touch. The whole thing had been strained, bordering on embarrassing, and it had been obvious to Karolina that none of the group had the slightest idea why they were spending time together.

The dinner at the National Museum was a formal occasion; everyone was in their finery, looking rich. Karolina had worn a simple dress, as she invariably did when Karl Johan took her to one of his events; she was always afraid of feeling vulgar among the blasé guests, who were mostly made up of wealthy individuals for whom art was a hobby.

The first thing that struck her when she met the man sitting next to her at the table was that he didn't really fit in; nor did he seem entirely comfortable. He clearly didn't feel right in his suit either, in spite of the fact that he looked very good: he was tall, broad-shouldered, with honey-blond hair that was thinning slightly on top, which kind of suited him. He gave an impression of manliness, in a way that was uncommon among men in the cultural sphere. When they had said hello—his name was Anders—and started talking, she understood why. He was a building conservation engineer and worked on restoration projects, he explained in a pleasant voice; she picked up a faint northern accent. As the evening progressed she became increasingly charmed by the fact that he was both a skilled craftsman, so skilled that he had been given the task of leading the restoration of the museum, and also an educated man, curious, well-read, with an interest in culture. At the same time, he was ordinary. She couldn't come up with a better word than ordinary. He reminded her of the guys she had known when she was growing up, guys who could whittle and paint and fix stuff that was broken, honest, unaffected, always ready to smile.

He radiated something she thought was perfect, although the wine might have had something to do with her opinion; he had a down-to-earth self-confidence she hadn't encountered in a man since she moved to Stockholm. He was funny too, in a toned-down kind of way; she couldn't remember when she'd last enjoyed herself so much. He told her that he ran his own company, that he had a wife and two children, she didn't really hear that or she chose to ignore it, a house in Älvsjö, she discovered that he smelled fantastic when she leaned closer to hear what he was whispering to her as a baroque ensemble played an extended piece before coffee was served.

She found it a little irritating when Karl Johan came over to ask her something. She introduced the two men and couldn't help comparing them: next to Anders, Karl Johan looked like a wimp.

Anders had to leave straight after dinner; he mumbled something apologetic about the babysitter, but she could see that he would have liked to have stayed. She stood up at the same time as him, said that she ought to leave as well, although she didn't give a reason. She asked him to wait a moment while she had a word with Karl Johan, who was trying to amuse the woman sitting beside him with anecdotes from his college days. Karolina told him she had a headache and was going home, but that of course he should stay. "Enjoy yourself!" she said warmly to show that she really didn't mind, to make absolutely certain that he wouldn't insist on coming with her.

She and Anders walked down the stairs, away from the hum of conversation. She could still recall it with absolute clarity; it was as if those few moments lasted for an eternity: their footsteps echoing on the marble as they walked through the foyer to the cloakroom, where a bored teenager handed them their jackets, out onto the steps where the reflections of the Royal Palace and the buildings of the Old Town shimmered in the sparkling waters of Strömmen, like a painting by Eugène Jansson; she was pleasantly drunk, and as they set off toward the taxi stand outside the Grand Hotel, she was seized by a desperate desire for something to happen.

"Couldn't we just..." she said, without knowing how the sentence was supposed to end; she could see in his eyes that he would agree to whatever she suggested. The cabs were no more than a hundred yards away, there wasn't much time.

"Couldn't we just go down here for a minute," she mumbled, taking his arm and leading him into a side street next to the Lydmar Hotel, where the darkness immediately swallowed them. She couldn't remember who kissed whom, they were drawn together, they almost swallowed each other in a series of utterly uninhibited kisses. The experience of kissing someone had never felt so perfect. They looked at each other and started laughing, surprised, delighted, then he kissed her again and she thought it was too good, so bizarrely good, as if they had been made to kiss each other.

"I have to see you again," he had said before he got into a cab. She had given him her number and they had met for a few drinks a week or so later after he had finished the class he was teaching at the Royal Academy of Fine Arts. The evening had ended the same way, with hungry kisses in the darkness; she was so turned on by the smell of him, by his lips and his hands, that her whole body was shaking as she quickly popped a couple of throat lozenges in her mouth and caught the subway home to Karl Johan.

They had embarked on an affair, so conventional that it could have served as the dictionary definition. They met in hotel rooms whenever they could find a window or come up with a convincing lie; it was more difficult for him, because he had a family and lived outside the city center. Karolina could always say she was working; Karl Johan had never questioned the fact that she was where she said she was going to be.

It certainly wasn't the first time she had been unfaithful, nor was it the first time since she had been with Karl Johan, but this was completely different. It turned out that she and Anders were as passionately well-matched in bed as their kisses had been; it was so staggeringly good that she started thinking, "Is this what it's all about?" because the risk that she might have missed out on the experience felt like a cruel, immense injustice. She had never had such incredible sex, she had never known such all-consuming intensity. She forgot herself, she was obliterated, and afterward she was left in a state of total relaxation and harmony. As she cuddled up close to his body, she would think that even if the sex was fantastic, this intimacy was almost better.

She loved lying by his side; his strong arms, the upper part covered in tattoos of ships and anchors, turned her on. None of the men she had known since her teenage years had had tattoos, and she followed their contours with her tongue, her fingertips. She would fall asleep with her head on his chest, in a state of deep calm; when she woke she felt slow and drowsy, her limbs entangled with his. Sometimes she pictured this closeness like a scene from a sci-fi film, two organisms living off each other, suckling each other with the most concentrated sense of intimacy she had ever experienced.

The generation of closeness was one of humanity's genuine mysteries, and a beautiful one, so primal, so tremulously intimate: the tacit agreement to lie there side by side, as true before each other as possible. When she lay next to Anders everything felt true in a way that nothing had felt true before. In those moments she loved him. You cannot rest within another person like this unless there is love, she thought. It wouldn't feel like this, as if her skin had been stripped away.

She recalled the time that followed as her halcyon days. Ever since she had first heard of the Greek myth in which the expression originated, she had loved it. Alcyone, the daughter of Aeolus, the god of the winds, and her beloved had angered the gods, and as a punishment she was turned into a kingfisher, the most beautiful of water birds. Out of consideration for his daughter, Aeolus restrained his winds for one week each December, when the female birds laid their eggs in nests on the shore. The waves were calmed, the whole of nature was peaceful.

The Greeks had used the expression "halcyon days" in other contexts, to describe periods when life was suffused with serenity and clarity. Karolina regarded this as the very epitome of the classical ideal, a symbol of antiquity and its harmony, its noble simplicity and quiet greatness, a peace as pleasant as an archaic smile. When she was with Anders, life suddenly seemed so simple. Nothing else mattered; the air seemed easier to breathe, her mind was at rest, just like the winds in the myth of Alcyone.

One evening they had both lied to their respective partners, telling them they had to work. They were lying sated beneath cool, smooth hotel sheets sharing a bottle of Burgundy she had brought with her; it tasted wonderful, even from the scratched Duralex glasses she had found in the bathroom. He talked about his mother; they had entered a new phase in their relationship, getting to know each other at a deeper level, which Karolina found immensely fascinating. It was like an extension of that primal, physical intimacy as she listened to him telling her things, opening up, making himself vulnerable. These moments felt like a remarkable gap in both time and space, where nothing that was said would have consequences, because they had no future plans, no everyday life waiting for them where every word could be used against them. There was only the present, and a total honesty.

His mother had died five years earlier, after a long illness. It had been a terrible period for the whole family, and it had taken its toll on him. He had found it particularly difficult to witness a whole series of deficiencies in his mother's care, which he described in detail: being discharged from the hospital too early, which resulted in grave consequences, doctors who didn't take her condition seriously enough, a terrifying lack of resources. He said he ought to have let the matter go by this stage, moved on, but that it was so hard. So many things had gone wrong; his mother might have pulled through, or at least had a few more years, and he was still angry. This anger had hardened into bitterness inside him; it still haunted him, flared up sometimes, and he didn't like to see the person it had turned him into.

He wept as he spoke and Karolina held him; she knew that his tears came not only from grief, but from relief at being able to confide in her without being afraid that he would frighten her away with sides of himself that he was ashamed of and found repulsive.

He stopped crying after a while, pulled himself together and looked at her with gratitude in his eyes.

"That was when I started voting for the Swedish Democrats," he said.

At first she thought it was a joke—an odd joke in the circumstances, but maybe he felt exposed and wanted to lighten the atmosphere. So she laughed. An awkward, confused laugh, and she stopped immediately when she saw that it was no joke. It was a continuation of his openness.

"Sorry," she mumbled.

"I know what you're thinking," he said quietly.

"You really don't."

At that moment she was actually thinking that he was wonderful. That it was bizarre to let go of such a genuinely good person even for a little while, to let him go home to a relationship in which he clearly wasn't happy, and to do the same herself, when it could be like this. It could be like this all the time: a state of total, all-consuming intimacy.

What did it matter if he had voted for a nationalist party a few times? The banality of it almost made her laugh again, the dwindling insignificance of his choice set against everything she felt for him. It simply provided a further level of closeness, another confidence like those they had shared about fears and childhood memories and sexual fantasies.

She asked him to tell her more, and he did. He had voted for the Social Democrats all his life, until his mother's illness. The devastating experience of the care system had been an eye-opener for him, and he had realized he was disappointed not only in the health sector, but also in the care of the elderly, education, housing, the way everything had gone.

"It's much harder to be an ordinary person who wants to work and get along," he said. "I don't care about anyone's skin color, I don't dislike people from other countries; I mean, I've studied and worked with people from all over the world. I just want society to function. I want our kids to learn something in school from teachers who know stuff, I want an orderly society, if someone gets sick I don't want them to have to put all their energy into fighting for decent care, I want everyone to have somewhere to live, even if they don't have hundreds of thousands of kronor in the bank and the ability to borrow millions...I'm in a good position, but I wonder what will happen to my kids. They're sensitive, they won't be able to fight for everything, and that's what you have to do these days if you're not rich. All the elements that automatically formed part of a decent existence in the past are gone. Suddenly we have people sleeping on the streets—we've gone back to the situation the Social Democrats and the welfare state tried so hard to get rid of. It's not right, it shouldn't be this way."

"No, it shouldn't. But do you seriously believe that voting for the Swedish Democrats will improve things?"

He shook his head.

"It felt right at the time," he said quietly. "I stood there clutching my voting slip, thinking that I hated what all the other parties had done. It felt like a revenge. I get it if you think I'm an idiot, but I just have a really strong impression that everything is going to hell."

She had reached the same conclusion for completely different reasons, but this shared view made her feel that he really understood her, that they were united in their view of the world. As she nestled closer, she thought she never wanted to let him go.

But it had all fizzled out anyway. Nothing to do with his political leanings, in fact she found it quite amusing; she didn't know anyone else who voted for the Swedish Democrats, and couldn't even imagine that any of her acquaintances might secretly do so. It was like the final taboo, something that could never be shared. How would it affect her if anyone found out? What would people at work say, people at the newspaper? The fact that he had told her was almost as big a deal as if he had produced an engagement ring.

Instead all of the boring practicalities of life came between them. It was the season for childhood ailments, and his family was constantly sick for a lengthy period; the winter vomiting bug and flu were passed on from one person to another, making it impossible for them to meet up. They were in a hotel room in Huddinge one afternoon when they had finally managed to find a couple of hours when they could be together, and he mentioned that his daughter had head lice. Karoline's scalp immediately began to crawl, she couldn't stop thinking about it. How would she explain it to Karl Johan if she got lice? Suddenly the whole situation was too complicated, too grubby and seedy, even though she was still desperate to see him, fantasizing about how it would be the next time they were alone, spending hours reliving their previous encounters in her head.

When the summer came he left Stockholm for several months, first of all for a long vacation in the South of France, then a few weeks with his in-laws on the west coast of Sweden. From there he sent her a long, agitated text one night: his wife had gone through his cell phone, read his saved messages and seen his pictures. Karolina knew at once that this was a disaster. Almost everything she had sent him, both texts and images, had been intended to turn him on.

"We can't meet up for a while," he had written; she hoped his tone was genuinely regretful. "I'll be in touch."

She hadn't heard from him again.

She had started sleeping late in the mornings since she left Karl Johan. She liked to stay up on Friday and Saturday evenings, lying on the sofa with her laptop watching a film, or pointlessly flitting from one social media site to another, getting annoyed about what her friends and acquaintances felt the need to update the world on. She didn't like adding her own posts—she hardly ever did anything special these days anyway—but she couldn't help observing others'. In fact, she could spend hours doing just that. She had Facebook and Instagram accounts where she virtually never posted anything herself, but silently followed hundreds of people, digesting their views on editorial writers and political debates, their everyday comments on sick kids and sports results, pictures of cozy Friday evenings at home and dinners with friends and nights out with the girls and summer cottages and birthday parties and pets. She knew where former classmates went on vacation, and she knew that Lennart Olsson, who lived alone but had a wide circle of friends, also had a large saltwater aquarium, full of apparently expensive and unusual fish.

She sipped several glasses of wine as the updates flickered by, contemplating all these worlds that were a distillation of the lives those around her were living, until eventually she slipped into a state that was a mixture of gratitude and resignation. Nothing anyone was doing really appealed to her, and yet she longed for exactly that, for normality and security. She always fell asleep with a sense of melancholy that persisted when she woke up. She often slept late, until eleven or twelve; she hadn't done that since she was a teenager. On top of the initial shame because half the day had gone, as her parents invariably pointed out when she lived at home, there was also an all-encompassing feeling of futility.

When she was with Karl Johan, it had been easier to believe that life had some kind of purpose. Someone had expected her to get up in the mornings, to provide company over breakfast, someone had wanted to hear her opinion on the latest twist in an ongoing debate in one of the morning papers. There had been a plan for the day, and even if it lacked any deeper meaning, it had still formed a framework on which to hang her life: there was shopping to be done, dinner to be planned, sometimes guests were coming, which involved housework and preparation, sometimes they were going to visit someone else, sometimes they were going to the theater or the opera, sometimes Karl Johan got it into his head that she needed to experience nature, in which case he would wake her early and they would find themselves standing in a forest in Södermanland before ten o'clock on a Sunday morning, where he could make the most of both his expensive Wellington boots and his very basic knowledge of birds and mushrooms.

She hadn't appreciated any of it very much at the time, but now that it was no longer there, she realized she missed it. Not necessarily Karl Johan, but she missed having someone to do perfectly ordinary things with, to make life seem not quite so pointless. These days she had to make a huge effort to find a reason to get out of bed on the weekends. Undertaking activities on her own—such as heading down to Fotografiska gallery, which was the most obvious destination if you lived where she did, a ten-minute stroll to Stadsgårdskajen—just made her depressed, because everyone else had company. When she did go out, she always felt as if people were giving her odd looks, judging her, speculating on what was wrong with her—why was she at Fotografiska all on her own on a sunny Sunday? She hated sunny Sundays more than anything nowadays, they were the most challenging days of all, when the angst was like a restless little animal, scrabbling around inside her head, stressed and confined.

It had taken a few months for the oppressive feeling of being a couple to turn into the oppressive feeling of loneliness.

When she was with Karl Johan, she had wanted to get away from the very thing she now longed for. Weekends in Vasastan had sometimes made her skin crawl; she had felt trapped, as if she had nothing of her own, as if she had become a part of a whole in a way that obliterated herself, when she didn't even know if she wanted to be a part of it at all. The essence of being a couple was a mystery to her. More than once she had thought she was incapable of such a relationship, because it never touched her deeply, as she knew it should. She had never felt that the words "I love you" meant what she instinctively knew they ought to mean in her relationship with Karl Johan. Yet she had said them often, and so had he, papering over the cracks in their everyday life. I'm working late, I won't be home for dinner, "I love you." Even the first time they said those words to each other, when they were young and had just fallen in love, she hadn't felt that "I love you" meant what it ought to mean. She had been unfaithful to Karl Johan many times during their years together, but above all she had deceived him with her lack of honesty toward him.

I have deceived everyone I have known, she often thought.

She had frequently sought refuge in her work. The claustrophobia that came with being part of a couple was largely responsible for her academic successes. If she had been blissfully happy with someone else, she would hardly have finished her dissertation by this stage. The reason why she and Karl Johan had lasted as long as they had was probably because he also worked long hours, and set great store by his social life. They just didn't see that much of each other.

When she needed a break from writing or marking test papers, she had gotten into the habit of strolling down to Åhléns City. She liked walking through Vasa Park and past Tegnèrlunden; even the soullessness of Drottninggatan filled her with an enjoyable melancholy if twilight was falling, or perhaps a little later when the worst of the crowds had dispersed. The department store stayed open until nine on weekday evenings, and after eight the place was virtually empty, suffused with a pleasant indolence. The staff knew they would soon be going home, and the professional mask slipped a little. It filled her with a warmth that reminded her of those occasions at elementary school when she had gone back in the evenings for a party or parents' evening or the St. Lucia procession in December. She had loved it so much: the darkness outside the windows, the empty corridors, so familiar in every tiny detail, yet suddenly different in the soft light, the stillness.

In Åhléns she could linger in the perfume department until she lost all sense of time, trying to decide which two perfumes she should try, one on each wrist. She could spend just as long in the changing room with a selection of clothes she had no intention of buying, clothes she wouldn't even have given a second glance during the day, when the lines of women waiting to try things on were long, and the shop assistants more pushy. She almost fell into a trance, warm and fuzzy, free from the need to think about anything other than which dress showed off her figure to its best advantage, or which shade of nail polish was the nicest.

She had started to regard those long, lazy visits to Åhléns as one of the joyful aspects of her life, until it occurred to her that perhaps that warm, fuzzy feeling wasn't happiness at all, but merely the absence of unhappiness. One meaningless activity replaced by another, which was slightly less painful.

It was when she realized that her everyday life was painful that she knew it couldn't go on.

.   .   .

Karolina!" Peter Tallfalk called out as she was passing his office. "Come here, I've got something to show you!"

He was holding up a book, John Ruskin's *Modern Painters* in a fine leather-bound edition. On the flyleaf was a bookplate, a bird of prey perched on the branch of a tree, with needles and pinecones in the foreground.

"Look!" he said, brimming over with enthusiasm. "It's my name—a falcon in a pine tree!"

She smiled.

"Lovely. Is it yours?"

He pointed to a pile of stickers on his desk, each adorned with the bird.

"I ordered them from a guy I know who does engravings. It's not exactly Dürer, but he is talented. I've always thought that a decent library should have a custom-made bookplate."

"Absolutely."

"I can give you his number if you like. And we should have that drink soon. Come over while the anemones are still in flower; they're beautiful at the moment."

"That would be lovely—how about Thursday?"

"Perfect."

She had just walked into her office when Anton Strömberg spotted her as he went past the door.

"Hi, how are things?" he said cheerfully.

She had noticed a few days earlier that he had been allocated one of the smallest offices farther down the corridor. He had to share with a female PhD student whose name Karolina could never remember. At the moment she was visiting a French university on an exchange program, leaving behind a battlefield of books and papers strewn across her desk. The surface of Anton's desk was still completely clear, except for a half-empty bottle of Coke.

The Department of Art History and Theory was made up of individuals who weren't particularly sociable, but who feverishly pretended they were, for example by organizing stiff, uncomfortable lunches every Wednesday, which Karolina usually tried to avoid. She loathed the mixture of superficial chat and careerist intrigue that inevitably characterized these occasions. Anton, however, seemed genuinely sociable.

"Fine, thanks," she replied politely. "Did you have a good weekend?"

As soon as she had asked the question, she realized it might be too personal. Whether or not he had had a good weekend was nothing to do with her. She imagined he had a wide circle of friends, that he had been to a party, flirted with some girl, maybe several, gone home with one of them. Woken up with a bit of a hangover, decided to stay in bed with her for half of Sunday too.

He shrugged.

"It was okay. I read most of the time. How about you?"

"Same."

She thought his wry smile looked appealing.

"Anything good?"

"I'm reading Rilke's letters about Cézanne at the moment," she said, in spite of the fact that she had barely opened the book. It had been lying on the pile by her bed for a long time. In recent months she had hardly been able to read at all, at least nothing that wasn't directly related to her work. In fact, she couldn't recall when she had last read a novel. Back in the spring? No—it was more like a year ago.

She was happy to read about apes; in fact, she looked forward to it. Yesterday she had learned more about Emmanuel Frémier, who had produced far more ape sculptures than the best-known piece, the gorilla abducting a woman. He had loved the tales the American explorer Paul du Chaillu wrote during his expeditions in West Africa in the mid-nineteenth century; they were filled with dramatic descriptions of his encounters with huge apes. Inspired by these accounts, Frémier produced a large sculpture for the Natural History Museum in Paris in 1895, entitled *Orangutan Strangling a Borneo Savage*. It was an enormous work, depicting an orangutan with a vicious look on its face sitting astride a handsome young man, its hands around his neck, egged on by a young ape. It represented the animal's violent triumph over man, a gladiatorial conflict frozen in marble. The young man had lost against his aggressor for over a hundred years, and would continue to do so.

Anton smiled at her lie about Rilke.

"Cool."

"How about you?"

"I'm kind of trying to find my way through what's been written about Symbolism, see what I can use," he replied hesitantly and a little evasively, which could mean that he was lying, and that her speculation about his weekend activities had been on the money. He had wandered into her office and sat down on the visitor's chair; he was looking at her in a way that conveyed polite interest and openness. He seemed to be expecting something from her—a follow-up question, or something else?

"I'd really like to see some of the pictures you're intending to use," Karolina said.

"Sure. Absolutely."

"Could you bring them to your first session?"

"The thing is . . . they're still with Ebba Ellis's relative."

"But that's not where you're working?"

"No, I have photographs of most of her paintings."

"Okay, good. In that case perhaps you could bring the photos?"

He took a deep breath, or was it a sigh? It annoyed her.

"I'm sure you have some excellent material," she went on patiently. "But you must understand that you can't base your dissertation entirely on correspondence. You have to have relevant pictures. That's what separates the art expert from the historian: we focus on aesthetic objects, and treat them as such in their own right."

Anton looked worried. Maybe he didn't like the fact that she was talking to him as a PhD student rather than her equal, which she found amusing.

"Judging by what I've seen of Ellis, she's a very interesting artist, but it's my responsibility to make sure you don't spend years of your life on something that's merely peripheral and irrelevant, so I would like to see more of her work. I really have no idea what you've been doing for a whole year. I'd also like to see what you've written so far; could you e-mail it to me before we next meet?"

"Okay."

He was tapping his pen rapidly and repeatedly on the arm of his chair, and it was getting on her nerves.

"Could you stop doing that," she said, a little more sharply than the situation merited. He was so surprised that he dropped the pen, which landed at her feet. She picked it up and gave it back to him. It was black, with an advertisement on the side: Elite Hotel Linköping.

"Are you from Linköping?" she asked, even though she already knew the answer. It was a stupid question anyway; surely it was more likely that he would have stayed in a hotel somewhere else rather than in his hometown? Fortunately he didn't appear to notice.

"My mom works there."

"In Linköping?"

"At the hotel."

Karolina nodded.

"She used to be a cleaner there when I was little," he went on. "I'd go to work with her sometimes. They had little tablets of soap wrapped in plastic, it shimmered like mother-of-pearl, and I was allowed to play with them. Lux, that's what it said on the label. These days they have..."

He caught her eye and suddenly looked embarrassed, as if he had given away something too personal.

"...soap dispensers fixed to the wall. And my mom works in reception," he concluded hastily.

She gave him what she hoped was an encouraging smile. That tiny insight into his background had been quite moving; she had assumed that someone with his self-confidence came from a family of academics, a tradition of feeling comfortable in a university environment. All at once she was ashamed of having been so hard on him.

"I'm from Gusum," she volunteered. "That's not far from Linköping."

He smiled. "Gusum is even worse," he said cheerfully. "Shit. Respect!"

She laughed. The atmosphere in the room had changed completely; suddenly she felt close to him. She knew it was a treacherous sensation, and she also knew that her imagination often took over. Her ability to empathize quickly with other people was the quality that had most frequently led to her being hurt.

Anton stood up. "I'll show you the pictures. On the eighteenth—isn't that when we're due to meet?"

She hadn't made a mental note of the date of his first mentoring session, but she nodded anyway.

"Cool. This is going to be fantastic," he said before disappearing through the door.

She wasn't sure if he was referring to his dissertation or her involvement in it, but whichever it might be, she was left feeling energized.

Roughly every two months she wrote an article for *Svenska Dagbladet*, according to a verbal agreement that she was one of their regular contributors. From time to time she wondered why they kept her on, given that she wrote so little and wasn't exactly a high-profile name. The only explanation she could come up with was the fact that Hans Jerup, the Danish arts editor who had taken over a few years ago, really liked her. He had made a point of talking to her at the events for freelance staff she had attended; he was cheerful and lighthearted, almost flirtatious. He was the kind of man she found it easy to be with, considerably easier than most men at the university. The choreography of heterosexual interaction was incredibly simple for her; it was more difficult when the men refused to play along. She often thought that just as some women were particularly good with children or animals, her forte was dealing with heterosexual men.

She also wrote features, usually on the newly published biography of an artist, or a review of an exhibition, occasionally a more provocative piece with its starting point in her area of expertise, which she described as visual art at the turn of the last century, with the emphasis on the portrayal of women. The same issues flared up at least once a year: the woman on this advertising poster was too skinny, the one in this TV series was too passive, the girl in this music video was too overtly sexy. She was bored with this type of discussion, but Jerup would always contact her and try to persuade her to come up with something.

Karl Johan had talked her into setting up a separate company for her freelance work, even though she couldn't really see the advantages. He had talked at length about all the tax deductions she would be able to make, but it rarely came to more than the odd magazine or book purchase, the occasional trip, a few cab fares, sometimes a lunch or dinner. Karl Johan had been much better at that kind of thing, buying antiques that were apparently essential for his working environment: a beautiful desk lamp with a green shade, a Chinese lacquered wastepaper bin, even an umbrella stand (how come the tax office went along with the idea that he needed an umbrella stand in his study?), and an Empire-style desk set that he loved to use, which included an inkwell and a pen with a steel nib. The whole thing began to irritate her after a while. At first she found it charming and unworldly, an expression of his eccentricity, which was an aspect of his personality that she had fallen for right from the start, but then it joined the list of things that got on her nerves. "Why can't you use a fucking biro like everybody else!" she had wanted to yell at him, but she hadn't done it. They had rarely quarreled.

In spite of the fact that she didn't have many receipts, she always panicked as the time to send the relevant paperwork to her accountant approached each quarter. She was always late. She had gotten into the habit of rushing down to the last-minute mailbox by the Klaraberg Viaduct with the envelope, always with a sense of immense relief at having achieved something important.

Dusk had begun to fall when she took the subway from Slussen to T-Centralen. The station echoed emptily and there was an air of late summer indolence and approaching desolation, with only a few passengers wandering around. The stores were closing, and the smell of French fries lingered. A Roma woman was sitting on a bench, begging from the passersby in a monotonous tone of voice. I never feel less like a resident of Stockholm than when I'm at Centralen, Karolina thought. People who didn't live in the city always ended up here, somehow believing that this was the heart of everything.

She remembered what it had been like when she still lived in Linköping: the trips to Stockholm to visit friends or go to a gig, always with the central station as their starting point, the toilets, the broken machines that were supposed to supply change for the left luggage lockers, all the logistics. And all the emotions a few years later, when it became synonymous with hope-filled arrivals or long, drawn-out goodbyes, when she starting coming into the city to meet boyfriends. First Joakim, who was going to be a psychologist; the mere thought of him kick-started a film-strip clattering through her brain, a series of miserable Sundays. Days characterized by a mixture of a hangover and her impending departure from the moment they woke up, wrapped around each other in his narrow bed in his student lodgings. They would buy pizza, sit in silence on the subway to the central station, kiss on icy platforms with lips that carried the bitter taste of coffee and smoke.

And later, a more adult relationship with Karl Johan, who had already started his doctorate and could afford to take her to restaurants and to the theater. Sometimes they would buy something on a Saturday as they wandered around the antique shops, with the tacit understanding that it would one day form part of the décor in their shared home. But there were still those messy, tearful departures, those same kisses on the platform, that same mixture of resignation and despair. Her eyes pricked as she thought of all the Sundays, all the goodbyes.

By the time she reached the viaduct, the entire city felt subdued, muted by the pink, misty twilight. A woman in a red woolly hat was standing by the mailboxes, muttering to herself.

"They've changed the collection time to five o'clock!" she called out to Karolina as soon as she spotted her; the look in her eyes was slightly alarming. "They've changed the fucking time to five o'clock!"

She was right. The mailboxes that had been emptied at nine o'clock for as long as Karolina had lived in Stockholm were now emptied at five, apparently, with absolutely no regard for the problems this might cause the post office's customers.

Her last-minute dash with the envelope full of receipts had been completely pointless. A wave of utter hopelessness washed over her, a childish feeling of disappointment, of not having gotten what she deserved in spite of her efforts. How come she couldn't even manage something so comparatively simple? How come she was so incapable of sorting out her life?

"Do we really have to put up with this?" the woman in the red hat shouted.

Karolina shook her head. Suddenly she felt like an integral part of the windblown, directionless individuals who found themselves in the area around the central station in the evenings. People who don't really have the ability to plan their lives, who need one last chance to pick up their medication from the duty chemist, to buy something for breakfast the next day from the 7-Eleven after every other store has closed.

"It's outrageous!" she said to the woman in the hat, whose face lit up.

"Outrageous!" she agreed.

Karolina told the story to Peter and Leyla Tallfalk the following evening, but it didn't come out quite right. With hindsight she thought it was both amusing and moving, but maybe she just came across as tragic. Maybe she actually was tragic, one step away from living in the gutter, wandering around the city in a woolly hat and shouting at people.

Peter and Leyla lived in the area known as Siberia, in a spacious ground-floor apartment with a small, private garden. When they showed it to Karolina she could understand why Peter liked to talk about it; if she had owned a place like this, she would have gone on at length to everyone she knew.

They had eaten on the wooden decking beneath a horse chestnut tree, its ripening fruits hanging from the branches like tiny medieval maces. The early autumn evening was cool, but infrared heating meant it was warm enough to sit out. Leyla had made her apologies and gone indoors to finish off a piece of work. She was a translator; maybe she really did have to work, but Karolina couldn't help thinking there was something else going on.

All around them the Japanese anemones and asters were flowering, the final exhalation of the summer. Whenever Karolina saw asters she thought about a poem by Stefan George, which contained a line about not forgetting the last pale asters in a garland of late summer flowers. The ones in Peter and Leyla's garden were not pale, they were strong shades of purple and cerise; even though they looked almost black in the darkness, you could still sense the depth of color, whatever the point might be—summer was over, after all. It was futile to show off like that at this time of year—a sublime futility, but that didn't make it any less ridiculous. Soon the night frosts would come.

Peter topped up her glass and cleared his throat.

"So what actually happened between you and Karl Johan?" he asked, just as Karolina had expected. She could tell from the tone of his voice that he'd been working up to it for a long time.

He knew exactly who Karl Johan was. Stockholm's art world was relatively small, divided into subgroups centered on museums, galleries, auction houses, academies, journalism and those employed by the state, but their paths constantly crossed. Karl Johan had moved in most of these circles, knew people in all of them. He and Peter had met at several exhibitions and viewings prior to auctions. She had never thought they liked each other much. Karl Johan had once said in passing that he thought Peter was boring, and Peter, who was too polite to say anything negative about Karl Johan in front of Karolina, had probably thought he was self-obsessed and superficial.

"I just knew our relationship was completely dead," she said. "We were lying in bed one night when I realized I felt completely indifferent toward him, and that I hadn't been excited about the future for a long time. And I started thinking how sad that was. When you're my age, you ought to be looking forward to the future. You are, aren't you? With Leyla?"

Peter nodded. "Absolutely."

"You have plans, things you want to do?"

"We're talking about buying a summer cottage. Leyla wants a bigger garden than this one, so we might try to find somewhere cheaper to live in the city so we can afford a cottage as well."

"Exactly—that's the kind of thing couples do when they're happy together. Karl Johan and I never made any plans. We never talked about the future. Once I'd realized that, I started to see him with different eyes. He seemed like a stranger, and I couldn't even understand why we were living in the same apartment. And I also knew I wasn't in love with him, not even a little bit. I'm not sure I ever was..."

Peter's expression was sympathetic.

"I don't know why it took me so long," Karolina went on. "Why I couldn't see that it was over. I should have finished with him ages ago, met someone else, gotten myself a house and a garden, had kids...I feel like such a failure, as if I've wasted years that I can never get back. Particularly as I'm a woman, and that damned...biological clock is ticking away."

"Failure is merely a question of perspective. What seems like a failure to you right now won't feel the same when time has passed. Maybe something good will come out of this. Not all men who can build a house can rebuild a ruin, as they say."

"I've never heard anyone say that."

"It has been said."

Peter gave her a warm smile; the conversation had brought tears to her eyes. Self-pity, she told herself. It's just self-pity. Stop wallowing.

But it was so hard. The memories of the years with Karl Johan were like quicksand, holding her fast until she was afraid of being sucked beneath the surface. How had they managed to carry on for so long? Why hadn't she become aware at an earlier stage that it wasn't a good relationship, why hadn't she simply walked away? Gone to one of the other men she could have chosen, particularly at the beginning when she was still young and attractive, when there was no joint bank loan to worry about. Somehow she had always known that what she had with Karl Johan wasn't what she really wanted, and yet she had stayed.

For example, right from the start it had bothered her that he didn't seem particularly interested in sex. Their sex life hadn't exactly been exciting to begin with; once they moved in together, it soon became virtually nonexistent. If they were watching a film or a TV series containing a sex scene, the atmosphere on the sofa was strained, as if they were both holding their breath while trying to look completely indifferent to what was happening on the screen, until the scene was over and they could relax and breathe normally again. They never discussed the issue; she didn't know what to say. It was no good complaining about the lack of sex when she wasn't even sure if she wanted it, but his lack of interest made her uninterested in him. She stopped seeing him as a sexual being and began to think of him as something else, a person she lived with but was never intimate with. Sometimes she had wondered if he was actually into women at all, or if she was part of a marriage of convenience without having been let into the secret. Then she thought it was probably because they were both unfaithful on a regular basis. He had once called her Ellinor, although they didn't know an Ellinor, and none of his previous girlfriends had had that name. From then on she had regarded their relationship as a kind of drama; they had reached the Mannerist phase, she thought, where it became a caricature of itself, to the extent that in the end nothing remained of the original concept.

"I remember he once talked about marriage, because an old friend of his had decided to tie the knot," she said. "I almost panicked; I knew that if we got married, I wouldn't be happy on my own wedding day. How sad is that?"

Peter shook his head.

"For better or worse..." she murmured. "We didn't even have much of a sex life."

Peter couldn't look her in the eye, and she realized she had perhaps been too frank. He was no prude; she hadn't met many prudish art historians. A field where naked bodies were the norm wasn't ideal for individuals with that level of sensitivity. However, he was reserved when it came to expressing his emotions, and in what he shared with other people. She had always liked that. She preferred his approach to those who loudly insisted on revealing every bit of themselves; she found their frankness irritatingly programmatic. In fact, she liked everything about Peter, even his slight gray appearance. In the subdued glow of the lamps on the decking, it was almost attractive, warm and friendly.

"Why can't I meet someone like you?" she said. "Someone I could have married."

"Karolina..."

His tone was kind, and she felt the tears pricking at her eyes.

"Sorry, Peter. I've had way too much to drink."

He smiled. "Shall I call you a cab?"

"Stop being so goddamn nice."

She slept late the next morning and woke feeling a little the worse for wear. The sun was blazing down mercilessly, it was hot, she was thirsty, and she'd run out of orange juice. She would die if she didn't get some juice. Maybe they had some small bottles at the gas station across the road.

There was a man waiting by the crossing on the opposite side, stabbing angrily at the button then staring at the sparse traffic. In a single movement he pulled off the dark blue sweater he was wearing over a bright green polo shirt. For a few seconds his stomach and chest were exposed to the whole street, even though there weren't many people around to see. A stab of both irritation and arousal shot through Karolina's body; it was hard to distinguish between them. Such self-confidence—to show such a large part of one's body without a hint of embarrassment. An imperfect body, his belly was big, quite fat really, and yet there was something attractive about it. He was deeply tanned, he had bushy blond hair and expensive sunglasses; what was he doing in this part of town? Maybe he was on his way to visit his mistress. She pictured him sitting in a motorboat in the summer, laughing out loud, his belly wobbling, his forehead shiny with sweat as he opened a beer. "You drink too much!" his wife snapped, she was also blonde and attractive, aged with pleasure and Botox and Pilates, two spoiled sons playing war games on their iPads, bored to death.

Yes, there was something exciting about men like that. She imagined having sex with him; for some reason they ended up at the same party, they were drunk, she'd been flirting with him all evening, more and more shamelessly as time went on, he would take her in the kitchen with her sitting on the countertop, he wasn't a very good lover but the whole situation turned her on so much that she came almost immediately.

Feminism has done a good job there, she thought, albeit unconsciously and with the aim of achieving the polar opposite: in this most secular and liberated age, it has created fresh taboos that she enjoyed using as the basis for her fantasies. She wanted to give her body to men who definitely didn't deserve her mind.

She bought three bottles of juice and drank two of them as soon as she got home. Then she went and stood in front of the bathroom mirror and attempted to improve her appearance with the aid of makeup. The light wasn't great, but she decided her reflection looked okay. When she was younger she had hated her appearance and believed she was ugly; she was less critical these days, although she could see from old photographs that she had been prettier back then. Time had passed so quickly. Had there been a gap between those last spots of her youth, which had hung around until she was well into her twenties, and the invasion of the wrinkles? She had no recollection of any such time, a time when she could have been happy with her face, met the world with pride, displayed it in the way she saw teenage girls showing themselves off every day in the late summer warmth: smooth, endless legs in the briefest of denim shorts, tanned, somehow open faces.

These days she faced the world with a mixture of resignation and confidence, which she could at least appreciate; this is what you get, her face said. It was one of the more positive aspects of growing older—the ability to feel relaxed. And she still looked good for her age; she was well-groomed and she took care of herself. Her face was harder, her body softer; that was how she had aged.

She blinked at her reflection, then applied a thin layer of foundation until her skin tone was sufficiently smooth and even. In the past she had tried to add dark contours to a round, girlish face that needed structure; now she tried to bring light. She had a fantastic primer that contained something called pearl powder, which gave her a glow, a radiance. It was absolutely essential nowadays. She used it every day, and worried constantly that the company would stop making it. However, if that happened, no doubt an even better primer would hit the market. She was prepared to spend a lot of money on skin care products.

She had recently paid around two thousand kronor for a cream that contained snake venom. It produced a mild allergic reaction which caused the skin to plump up just enough to make the wrinkles less prominent and to create a smoother impression. She didn't have all that many wrinkles, and she knew that the reason behind such things was largely genetic, but she was still pleased that the area around her eyes was comparatively unlined, having used expensive eye creams since the age of twenty-five. She liked to invest in skin care, liked the idea that a defense against physical deterioration was there, packaged in beautiful jars and boxes and tubes, as long as she was willing to pay.

In Karl Johan's circles, among rich men with rich wives, she had always felt rather pale and washed-out. There was something strikingly unnatural about the perma-tanned upper-class women with their eyelid lifts and lip fillers, but she found their refusal to let themselves be defeated by nature strangely appealing.

It was different at the university and in the world of the cultural media in which she sometimes moved. Excessive vanity was frowned upon if you wanted to be taken seriously. It was just about okay to dress up for a party, but not for everyday life. In her department most people shuffled around in clogs, and the kind of clothes she personally wouldn't even wear to go down to the laundry room: baggy jeans and bobbled sweaters. It was impossible to imagine any of her female colleagues going for a boob job.

The same applied to the women attending the launch party at Rönnells antiquarian bookshop, she thought a few hours later. Lennart Olsson had invited her; he had contributed to a new anthology on aesthetics, a joint project undertaken by a number of higher-education institutions, and he had taken part in an open discussion which Karolina had listened to with half an ear. The place was packed, and as she glanced around at the people standing there, clutching a plastic glass of bag-in-the-box wine, she was well aware as usual that she had no interest whatsoever in this world. As far as she was concerned, those who moved in cultural circles were something she just had to put up with because she enjoyed reading and writing. She was sure that many of tonight's guests felt very differently; the real appeal for them lay in what was going on right now among the bookshop's shelves. She recognized plenty of faces, some from the academy, some from pictures accompanying their byline on the arts pages of the newspapers. Many were young with their gaze fixed on a career in arts-related media, faithfully turning up at this kind of event, not least because they could get drunk for free, but also because it was an opportunity to make contacts, to talk their way into a commissioned article in a newspaper or journal. And there was always the chance of an after-party, sometimes at Lennart's house.

Maybe he would invite people back today. He was surrounded by wide-eyed young men who couldn't be more than twenty-five, and equally wide-eyed young women in shapeless black clothes and big glasses, pretty thanks to their youth in spite of their appalling fashion sense. Strangely enough, Lennart seemed most taken with one of the men; Karolina thought there was something familiar about him, that loose, casual stance. When he turned around she saw that she had been right: it was Anton.

He spotted her at the same moment and beckoned her over.

"This is fantastic!" he said delightedly, giving her a warm hug. She hugged him back a little awkwardly, taken by surprise. Hugs weren't really appropriate in their relationship, but she could smell the wine on his breath, which probably explained his actions. She picked up something else too, maybe it was his fragrance; it was the same smell that he had left behind in her office, fresh and green.

Lennart gave her a strained smile. She had seen that smile before, and she knew it meant he didn't want her there. In his eyes, in the way he was gazing at Anton, she saw something that she knew was a kind of instant infatuation, although it was still platonic at the moment. Anton had somehow managed to impress him, perhaps just because of the way he looked.

She had understood early in life that attraction can take many forms. The most common usage of the concept, heterosexual attraction, was merely the tip of the iceberg of all the rootless, nameless desire contained in the world. The only word she could use for what she saw in Lennart's eyes was "desire."

"I was just telling Lennart about Ebba Ellis," Anton said enthusiastically.

"She sounds so interesting!" Lennart said.

The way he conferred his approval always provoked Karolina. Now that he had given Anton's topic his blessing, it was immediately interesting. When she had asked him about Ebba Ellis a few weeks ago, he couldn't have cared less.

"I know," she said. "But you'd never heard of her, had you?"

Lennart handled the situation well, she had to give him that. There wasn't a flicker to indicate that she was right.

"As I was saying to Anton," he said instead, raising his voice slightly, "the research he will be carrying out is immensely important. It reminds me of my own work on the modernists. We have so much left to do when it comes to rediscovering forgotten female artists."

"As I understand it," Karolina countered, "this is not so much a question of a forgotten female artist among many others, but a completely unknown artist, period. An artist whose imagery is totally unique in the history of Swedish art, and who was in close personal contact with the international art scene. The subject is interesting in itself, not because we happen to be talking about a woman."

"As I said, Anton will be looking at an extremely important feminist body of work."

"I realize that's a key word when you're applying for grants, Lennart, but the fact that the artist is a woman doesn't make this feminist research."

"Karolina, I thought you'd be the first to appreciate the value of Anton's project!"

"Its importance has nothing to do with feminism, that's all I'm saying."

"It's important, that's all I'm saying."

"Nobody said it wasn't."

Anton was watching them, his expression amused.

"Lennart," he said, finishing off the last of the wine in his plastic glass. "I hear your after-parties are legendary."

And so she found herself standing in Lennart Olsson's kitchen, still with its original décor: 1940s functionality and Formica worktops on which bottles of wine and a bowl of chips had been laid out. In the spacious living room the walls were largely covered in bookshelves, interrupted only by one wall on which most of Lennart's art collection was displayed. It consisted of female artists, whose work had increased in value thanks to the hours of research he had put in while being paid by the state.

The impressive saltwater aquarium took center stage in the room, spreading a harsh, cold light all around it.

"Don't feed the fish!" Lennart said loudly, as if he were reprimanding a class of badly behaved schoolchildren. "Last time the aquarium was contaminated with crushed-up chips!"

Anton snorted with laughter; he was obviously drunk.

"Haven't you got some kind of snail or fish to keep it clean, Lennart?" he asked loudly.

"They're too expensive, and they're not supposed to eat chips," Lennart replied wearily.

Anton laughed again. "You should have a bookworm!" he chortled. It really was a terrible attempt at a joke, but he seemed delighted with it. He turned to the girl beside him, one of the pretty ones in shapeless clothes. "A bookworm!" he repeated. She smiled politely, then looked at Karolina.

"What beautiful earrings," she said quietly.

"Thank you."

She had bought them in a secondhand shop a long time ago; they were old, made of some kind of gold-colored metal. They dangled and tinkled when she moved her head, looking glamorous in a slightly cheap way that pleased her.

Suddenly the girl moved closer and touched one of the earrings with her fingertip.

"Fabulous," she said with her mouth right next to Karolina's cheek, her breath was warm.

"Thank you," she murmured again.

"My name is Moa."

"Karolina."

"I know. I know who you are." Moa didn't move; she was staring at her. "I really like what you've written. About dangerous women. It's incredibly inspiring."

Karolina had a fleeting vision in which the party went completely off the rails. If someone just took the initiative, Anton and Lennart and Moa would rip off their clothes and collapse in a tangle of flesh on the shabby Howard sofa; no doubt she would be expected to join in.

It was as if Moa had read her mind.

"Why don't we play truth or dare?" she suggested.

Anton and Lennart were very taken with the idea. Anton took a huge swig of wine, then grinned.

Did people really do this kind of thing? Was this really how book launches ended these days? Was she the one who needed to get out more?

"Truth or dare?" Moa said, fixing her gaze on Anton.

He thought for a few seconds. "Dare."

"Kiss someone in the room," Moa said firmly.

Karolina wasn't surprised when he put his arm around Moa, pulled her close and gave her a long kiss, to which she responded with enthusiasm. But something was bothering Karolina; what was it? Jealousy? Yes. Definitely jealousy. It was troubling to realize that she had wanted him to kiss her.

She glanced at Lennart, only to discover that he was already looking at her with an expression she had never seen before. It was so embarrassingly shameless that she had to lower her eyes. It wasn't hard to work out what he was thinking, and she found it unpleasant, almost shocking.

To tell the truth, she had never been all that choosy when it came to men. In the world in which she moved, most people were quite good-looking, or at least well-groomed and well-dressed; if they couldn't manage that, they were usually amusing or intelligent or interesting. In fact, it was hard to find a man who didn't have some redeeming features, and although she wasn't actively keen on too many of them, she wasn't actually repulsed by them either. Most were simply reasonably attractive, if you took an overview of their appearance and personality.

Lennart Olsson certainly lacked the classic male qualities that would have made him successful in a war, or as a defender of his flock on the savanna at the dawn of humanity, but she realized he could be regarded as attractive by women in a similar position who moved in the same circles. He had done comparatively well in his role both as an academic and as a writer. He had a wide network of contacts, and was a frequent guest at all kinds of cultural events. He always wore a jacket. He still had most of his hair.

And yet she felt a strong antipathy toward him, bordering on revulsion, which was unusual for her. The thought of being intimate with Lennart in any way made her genuinely uncomfortable. It was hard to put her finger on the real reason; maybe it was his aura, which seemed to her to be entirely gray, a manifestation of his lack of humor and self-awareness, his careerist opportunism, his self-image of a man who embraced equality, in spite of the fact that he constantly, and presumably unconsciously, took every opportunity to find fault with her. She had also heard rumors that he was just as supercilious with his students and PhD candidates, that he was careless and slipshod both as a teacher and as a supervisor, probably because he believed he was above such tasks.

That inviting look from him made her shudder. And then she got angry: What the hell was he thinking? Did he really imagine she would want to kiss him at a drunken party that had regressed to teenage idiocy, did he really think she would suddenly find him desirable? As far as Karolina was concerned, there was nothing desirable about Lennart Olsson, and there never would be.

What was she even doing here? She was too old for this nonsense. Thank God.

She stood up and said she had to head out. She ignored the protests and quickly put on her coat and shoes in the hallway. As she closed the front door behind her, she could hear the sound of muted laughter from the living room.

She walked to the Natural History Museum the following day and stopped in front of the imposing edifice. The main building with its dome was impressive, but it was the whole thing she loved, the wings framing the courtyard and creating a space in the center. As she stood there she thought it was as if the museum wanted to embrace her, as if it was holding out its arms in a loving but challenging way. It was a building in which she would have wanted to pray to a god. If she had believed in a god.

Once inside, having bought her ticket and pressed the little sticker onto her jacket, she wandered around slowly and aimlessly. It was lovely and cool; she gazed at the floors, and the shifting colors on different levels, the brown marble stairs with their elliptical white fossils, green marble higher up, shimmering as the light played over it. In a large room on the first floor there were heavy wooden benches under the windows, polished by the generations of visitors who had rested for a while after taking in all the collected scientific achievements presented within the walls of the museum. The place was almost deserted apart from the odd father on paternity leave with his small children, one or two tourists.

She spent a long time contemplating the dioramas of animals in the permanent exhibition on nature in Sweden. A pack of wolves, a family of elk, a bird table in winter, a fox with its back arched as it pounced on a mouse, a dramatically lit Ural owl that appeared to be staring at her. The exhibit had been taken from one of the books by Elsa Beskow that she had loved as a child, giving her a sense of security associated with preschool and elementary school, years when she learned a great deal about the world, but when the world remained small, concrete, comprehensible.

And she really did feel secure as she wandered around among the stuffed animals; she was comforted by the orderliness of it all, the desire to classify existence. This was the opposite of her own field of research, scientific order in contrast to emotionally driven art and decadence. Amiable, pedagogical efforts to explain the names of deciduous trees, how an anthill works, the passage of the seasons, things that simply go on. Things that will go on forever. There is no Mannerism in nature, at least not within a time perspective that we are capable of grasping. She contemplated a stuffed hedgehog. "The hedgehog is one of our oldest mammals," she read on an information board. "There were hedgehogs on the earth 65 million years ago!"

She tried to imagine sixty-five million years, but it was impossible. She had always found it difficult to get her head around both long periods of time and immense distances, it was as if her brain couldn't handle large numbers, yet at the same time she couldn't help thinking about them, even though the experience verged on self-torture. Distances in space were the worst, and could almost induce a panic attack.

For a while she had been obsessed with the disposal of nuclear waste after seeing a documentary about a facility that was being built in southwestern Finland. Spent uranium rods will be enclosed in copper capsules and buried in the granite bedrock, and around the year 2100, the facility will be sealed forever. One of the difficulties, apart from the possibility that the bedrock might leak, was how to make future generations or life-forms who might come across the entrance understand that they must stay away, leave it alone.

Karolina sat and googled the issue for several nights in a row; she read discussions in scientific forums and on blogs, utterly fascinated yet at the same time terrified by the mind-blowing thought of the distant future. It almost made her feel ill; she experienced a sensation of dizziness, as if she were standing on the edge of an abyss looking down, with time falling steeply away right in front of her, down into something abstract and incomprehensible over which she had absolutely no control.

The most ancient cave paintings were around thirty thousand years old; she had always thought that was a difficult time frame to imagine. It seemed so remote that the people who painted horses in caves might as well have been a different species. The pyramids were built four thousand five hundred years ago. Egyptian culture was totally alien to her; like the Greeks, she regarded it as barbaric, cold and bloodthirsty. Four thousand five hundred years on the earth was no more than the blink of an eye, a brief moment. The nuclear waste in Finland was to remain buried in the bedrock for at least a hundred thousand years.

The distant future became even more staggering when she started to delve into the suggestions and theories that were the result of research into the ways in which it might be possible to communicate to subsequent civilizations that the contents of the storage facility were lethal. Scientists, linguists and anthropologists had taken part in a major project initiated by the government of the United States in the 1990s when a similar storage facility was due to be built in Nevada. They had concluded that no existing symbols would be comprehensible within such a lengthy time frame. In addition, any kind of warning was open to the opposite interpretation; for example, it might be there to frighten off intruders because the contents of the facility were in fact valuable. She remembered the adventure movies she had seen as a child, the elaborate traps constructed to protect treasure in burial chambers and pyramids. There was simply no way of communicating with the future, and yet it was absolutely essential to do so.

The hedgehog gazed back at her through the glass display case. She had always liked hedgehogs because of the combination of their sweet little currant eyes and the sharp spines on their backs, and because they had survived for sixty-five million years and suddenly found themselves in the middle of modern civilization.

She spent a long time in the museum shop, still lost in the exhibition she had seen, and excited by the sea of scientific bits and pieces spread before her. When she was a little girl she had been unable to tear herself away, transported by all the things that were so different from the selection of toys available in Gusum. She had stood there for an eternity, carefully considering what she could buy with the pocket money she had saved. Her parents had had to hurry her along several times before she eventually chose a kaleidoscope. There were still similar ones on sale, cardboard tubes with colored chips rattling inside. She picked one up, put it to her eye and gazed at the patterns it made.

Then her attention was caught by the beautiful stones, minerals and crystals polished to a perfect finish. She ran her fingertips over a basket of rose quartz, cool and smooth. A larger basket contained ammonites; she rummaged around trying to decide which she liked best, weighing one in her hand. It was amazing that nature could create this, she thought as she traced the spiral which tapered off toward the tip. It reminded her of a nipple—in fact, the whole ammonite was like the essence of the female body, with the faint mother-of-pearl glow of its opening, breast and sex organ contained in the same object.

She loved men and their bodies, but from a purely aesthetic point of view, the female body was more beautiful, biologically and artistically perfect, superior. At the same time, women were a mystery to her. She understood men, they were simple. When she was growing up she had regarded herself as boring and ugly; as a young adult she suddenly found herself in situations where she was seen as attractive and interesting, and where she could often have whomever she wanted. She had quickly learned how to talk to men, make them laugh, ensure that they saw her as irresistible. She had enjoyed it; she loved men.

She had never spent a great deal of time with women; she hadn't had many girlfriends when she was younger, and now she had none. They had slowly disappeared, one by one, which is what happens as we grow older. Of the women she had hung out with at college, some had moved away and most had become mothers. Even if children didn't necessarily have to mean that the friendship had faded, it had just turned out that way. A lot of things in her life had just turned out that way.

She also thought it was more difficult to be with women; she still wasn't quite sure why, but perhaps it was because in her experience these encounters often led to a series of comparisons—of lives and careers and partners and families and appearance, where one party always felt the need to come out on top. She had no need to compete with men, they were completely different. She could relax in their company. Maybe that was why women were the subject of her research, in the hope that a scientific approach could enable her to understand something that life had kept from her.

After her dissertation, her next project had focused on women in film. She had produced a slim volume on the erotic thrillers of the late 1980s and early 1990s and their female protagonists. She put forward the view that the dangerous women in these movies could be seen as a resurgence of the femmes fatales in the paintings featured in her doctorate, the castrating vampire and Salome figures who had bubbled up in art at the end of the next century as well.

The book hadn't attracted many reviews, and the reception was mixed. The most positive was published in a feminist arts journal that approved of the content because it was written with great empathy for these women; maybe it could even be seen as a defense on their behalf. With hindsight Karolina thought she might have gone too far when she compared Glenn Close at the moment of death in *Fatal Attraction*, shot by her lover's wife and lying on the blood-stained tiles in the married couple's bathroom, with the crucifixion. "A Mary Magdalene without the obligatory epithet 'the penitent,' which less broad-minded times insisted on ascribing to her: this Mary Magdalene is allowed to live. Alex in *Fatal Attraction* dies because of the sins of the man who breaks his marriage vows, crucified in the nuclear family's newly purchased home in the suburbs." This passage was quoted appreciatively in the review.

She wrote the final chapter just after one of her own affairs had ended. She had been emotional, and afterward she thought it had been unscientific, but on the other hand: If no one had created anything when they were in an emotional state, how many good things in our history would not exist?

Funnily enough, the book, which she hadn't seen as being particularly significant, had been immensely beneficial when it came to her career. Just as it came out a professorship was advertised at the University of Linköping, specializing in the study of popular culture. It was actually the polar opposite of everything she liked and wanted to work on, and she would probably never have considered applying if Peter Tallfalk hadn't persuaded her. He had pointed out the job posting to her, discreetly nagged her for several weeks until he talked her into accepting the idea, then he had been a great help when it came to filling in the application. Peter was more than a little cynical after all the years he had spent at the university, but he also had a clear perspective on what worked. He had shown her how to sift out every sentence in her dissertation that referenced anything remotely approaching popular culture, he had dug deep in all the essays and articles she had written, searching for any mention of wider contemporary cultural phenomena, and in the end he had managed to transform her research into a consistent investigation into images of women in popular culture, a stringent, contemporary project with clear feminist influences, with the slim volume on women in film as the cherry on top.

To her surprise it had succeeded beyond all expectation. She didn't get the post in Linköping, but came a close second. And a year or so later, when a lectureship in the theory and history of art was advertised in Stockholm, she applied and got the job. She was automatically upgraded to professor.

At first she couldn't shake off the feeling that she had conned her way into the post, especially when she thought about how enthusiastic the department had been about her commitment to feminist perspectives within multimedia studies, but she soon stopped thinking that way. Instead she told herself that, with Peter's help, she had seen through the system and given it exactly what it wanted. She had just as much right to benefit from the mechanisms of academia as anyone else, and if she had presented her research as she herself saw it, she would never have progressed—Peter had made her realize that. She had no doubt that he was right.

She was embarrassed when she noticed that the assistant in the museum shop, a woman in her sixties, was watching her. She grabbed a few of the cool, smooth crystals, then paid for them along with the kaleidoscope and the ammonite, which the assistant carefully wrapped in tissue paper.

Back at her desk she took out the ammonite and placed it on the windowsill, then arranged the crystals in a group beside it. A little still life dedicated to the natural sciences, or perhaps an altar, a collection of relics with its mother ship, the Natural History Museum, providing a backdrop through the window. The thought put her in an unusually good mood.

She had never really enjoyed teaching, and she probably wouldn't have to do it if she didn't want to, but at the moment she was looking forward to the course on nineteenth- and early-twentieth-century art that she was due to run later in the semester. She had done it before and thought it was good, and above all it would give structure to her life. Right now she was at the mercy of her writing, and therefore her own brain, for most of the working week when she wasn't involved in meetings or supervising her PhD students.

The air in the corridors seemed stickier than ever, her colleagues' small talk more inane than ever. Before she started her doctorate she had imagined that the university staff would have truly intellectual discussions, but she had soon realized that it was a workplace just like any other, with the same topics of conversation: the weather, the weekend, the kids, TV programs, the contents of today's lunchbox. While she waited for the water from the faucet in the staffroom to get cold enough, she listened to two junior lecturers in the history of ideas as they shared a sandwich and chatted about what one of them should buy with a gift voucher from an electronics chain.

"Have you got a mixer?"

"I've got a stick blender."

"What about a good coffee machine? A Moccamaster?"

"I already have a coffee machine."

"The coffee tastes so much better with a Moccamaster."

"But they're so expensive—are they really worth the money?"

"If you don't know what to buy, I think you should invest in a Moccamaster."

She heard them as if they were some distance away; their conversation was like a background murmur, blending with the sound of the printer and the dust in the still air. It was hard to get the water cold enough. When it was acceptable, she drank standing at the sink, then refilled her glass and took it back to her office, where she swallowed a painkiller with the first gulp.

A whole pile of e-mails was waiting in her inbox: new chapters from a PhD student, suggested dates and times for meetings she had no wish to attend, an invitation to the leaving party for a secretary who was due to retire, a pretty no-nonsense woman who seemed to have worked there forever. Karolina's head felt hot, her mind restless. Neither the water nor the painkiller was helping.

She opened a new window and typed in the address of one of the porn sites she sometimes used. In a way it could be regarded as research, she told herself; after all, the focus of her research was images of women. The latest movies were listed on the home page: *Ebony honey gets it deep, Mature lesbian licking, Chubby teen swallows it all.* Anything would have done, as long as it felt like a taboo it was fine, and in her office everything was taboo. She chose a film with two men and one woman, a brunette with big breasts who was taken on a leather sofa by both men, who were generically porn-film handsome, unreal and therefore not particularly arousing, but the knowledge that someone could walk by in the corridor at any moment, maybe even knock on the door, meant that she came almost right away.

Afterward she hurried to the bathroom, her cheeks still flushed from the orgasm. When she got back to her desk it was easier to concentrate, and she opened up her notes on apes.

Her research had led her down all kinds of strange routes. She didn't really know how it had happened, but soon she had left art behind and found herself reading with interest about research on the periphery of the natural sciences. She was especially fascinated by the Russian biologist Ilya Ivanov, who had begun his scientific career by developing the practice of artificial insemination in cattle and racehorses. However, as early as 1910, at an international congress in Graz, he had presented his new goals. He wanted to go further than simply crossbreeding different animal species; his aim was to investigate the possibilities of creating a human-ape hybrid.

His ideas won support in the Soviet Union, which regarded scientific achievements, particularly those influenced by Darwinism, as tools against the peasantry, who in the eyes of the regime were far too religious. After lengthy negotiations Ivanov managed to secure a small sum of money, and permission to use the Pasteur Institute's research station in French Guinea. In November 1926 he arrived in Conakry, the capital city, along with his twenty-two-year-old son, a biochemistry student at the University of Moscow who was also called Ilya. The research station was located in the botanical gardens outside the city center, an area rich in tropical vegetation, with enormous trees and palms. The facility provided optimum conditions for Ivanov's research: the station specialized in primates, and could supply him with female chimpanzees.

Karolina pictured him in her mind's eye, a Soviet Dr. Frankenstein, or Moreau, or Faustus, standing outside his laboratory in the evenings. A small man with a well-groomed white beard, his lab coat a little on the large side. The heat and humidity of West Africa, the black night falling fast. The lab is a two-story building with a porch lit by paraffin lamps, mosquitoes flocking around them, a whining, flickering glow. Ivanov lights a cigarette, looks up at the building. Inside is his universe; in there he is God. That is where he creates life, new and hitherto unknown life-forms. That is where the line between man and animal ceases to exist, between human understanding of nature as a separate entity from culture, a final, critical taboo which will soon prove to be no more than a figment of the imagination of narrow-minded brains. "If we simply push a little harder against the door that separates man from other species," Ivanov thinks, "we will discover that it is not locked."

All his experiments fail. He commits what can only be described as a series of violent assaults on female chimps. His son has to go outside and vomit over the porch fence after witnessing the rape of a screaming female chimp in the name of science, and his father still doesn't manage to impregnate the animal with sperm donated by local men, chosen for their strength and fertility.

Ivanov and his son take a number of female chimps home; several die before they even arrive, and none of them falls pregnant. The surviving apes are placed in a new center by the Black Sea, set up specifically for research into primates. It is located in Sukhumi in western Georgia, one of the few places in the Soviet Union with a subtropical climate. However, they are still far away from the heat of West Africa; the chimps become ill.

Back home, new opportunities come to light. While he was in French Guinea, Ivanov had begun to consider a simpler alternative. Instead of attempting to impregnate female chimps, why not inseminate women with sperm from male apes? This option would require fewer apes, the whole thing would be a much more straightforward process, less expensive, less complicated.

The Science Academy wants nothing to do with the project, but the Communist Academy decides that it is in their interests to investigate the possibility of crossing man and ape. They feel that the human reproductive system ought to be separated from the bourgeois institution of marriage. In 1929 the Commissariat for the Interspecies Hybridization of Primates is founded. Only one of Ivanov's apes is still alive by this stage, a twenty-six-year-old male orangutan called Tarzan. It is deemed important to get the experiment under way as quickly as possible, and the search begins for women who are willing to participate. The word "willing" is key: those who volunteer for idealistic or ideological reasons rather than financial gain are likely to be more reliable, more prepared to refrain from sexual congress both before and after the experiment, in order to keep it "pure."

Ivanov refers to her as G in his notes. They exchange letters for a while. "Dear Professor," she writes. "Since my private life is in ruins, I can see no point in my continued existence. However, the idea of being able to make a contribution to science gives me the courage to contact you. Please do not turn me down. I would very much like you to consider me for your experiment."

G. Given the nature of the experiment, she should have been young, the perfect age for optimum fertility. And yet she must have been old enough to be disappointed in life. Old enough for her private life to have been ruined. By what? Or whom? A disappointment in love so devastating that she had given up all hope of a normal existence. A disappointment so catastrophic that the idea of sitting in a gynecologist's chair in a research laboratory by the Black Sea while a strange man attempted to inseminate her with an ape's sperm seemed like a reasonable option.

Karolina couldn't stop thinking about her. She googled Russian girls' names beginning with *G*, and decided on Gavriila. The female form of Gabriel, the archangel, who told Mary she would conceive and bring forth a son.

It was like one of Zeus's metamorphoses, only this time he had taken the form of an ape rather than a bull, a swan or a shower of gold. Receiving him was like becoming the Europa or Leda or Danae of the new age, and a refusal would be like saying no to immortality. Ivanov himself believed that his experiments had global significance, and were of vital importance for the whole of humanity; he thought his name would appear in history books all over the world for all eternity.

And a woman had indeed offered to carry an ape in her womb, to give up her body to a monster, a life-form that had never been seen before. It would grow inside her, she would nourish it, give birth to it. Perhaps she would kiss its forehead in a moment of strange maternal joy, this creature that would after all be half her. And half animal.

It was revolting, yet at the same time it somehow made sense. If there was one thing Karolina could understand, it was the longing for something to submit to, something bigger than oneself: science, art, religion.

Not to mention the feeling that life was in ruins. That was the word Gavriila had used: ruins. That was the word Karolina would have used too.

. . .

The Östra Söder region had started getting itself ready for the new subway line to Nacka; with its planned station at St. Sofia's church it would bring new life and rising property prices to a part of the inner city that had felt a little cut-off until now, because it wasn't part of the subway network. It would take many years to blast out the tunnel in the bedrock, noisy, dusty work that would probably drive Karolina crazy, but she still thought of her apartment as temporary, as a phase that would soon be over when her life got going again, when she was a stable person in a relationship built on the things that relationships ought to be built on: attraction, friendship, respect, intimacy, trust. Things that would form a solid basis for giving up her shabby apartment in Östra Söder and moving in with a partner.

A fierce debate about the St. Sofia station had erupted during the spring, when it became clear that one of the entrances leading down to the subway would have a classic design reminiscent of a small Greek temple. "An idiom fishing in murky waters," one writer had claimed; reading between the lines, it was clear that he believed there was something fascist about such a construction, and probably the architect who had come up with the idea, not to mention the contemporary ethos that adds fuel to the fire of such tendencies and then tacitly approves.

Karolina had definitely done just that, but with hindsight she had thought that she should have shouted at the top of her voice, used the space she could doubtless have secured in *Svenska Dagbladet* to say that it was an excellent plan. She really loved the architect's sketches, which had been published in conjunction with the debate, and even if she didn't know whether he was being serious or ironic in his use of classicism, she still thought it was a beautiful building. It had columns, and in her opinion people should be grateful for all the columns they got.

She thought the same every time she was in what was probably the worst place in Stockholm, the pedestrian tunnel between the commuter train station and the subway at Centralen. At least there were columns, or maybe they were actually pillars, tiled so that it was easy to clean off the graffiti and urine and whatever else might end up on a pillar in a place like that. They divided the crowds who poured through the tunnel virtually 24/7. She had read an article about it in a popular science journal; experiments with mice had shown that they behaved in exactly the same way. In a stressful situation, many people, or mice, wander in all directions and get caught up in a crush and trample one another underfoot. The pillars make the group instinctively divide: on the way to the commuter trains they keep to the left, following the stream of others going in the same direction. This benefits everyone, and is important for areas that need to be cleared quickly, according to the article. In an emergency, the limited ability to move forward means, paradoxically, that an evacuation can be achieved much faster.

Karolina liked all kinds of pillars, and she loved columns. If she had to choose just one object in Western cultural history, she would choose the column. She associated it with archaic purity, marble-white Greek temples, a Utopian classicism that she adored, even though it was hard to be open about such a view. Whenever she stood in front of classical columns, she felt as if a better world had been brought to life by them, a world of ideas, the essence of all that was good about the cultural heritage of the West. Classicism was the promise of something greater, something more beautiful. It was hardly surprising that the Nazis had chosen that particular idiom for their own, she often thought. If you measured yourself against classicism, you would always be found wanting.

She liked the pillars at Centralen because they reminded her of beauty, right in the midst of all those stressed-out commuters who gave way to the disabled and the lame, the poor and the wretched who gathered around the pillars. And the man who sold lottery scratch cards; he had been standing there ever since the fall of 1996 when she first arrived in Stockholm. He had aged. Which meant she had too.

Over the past few months she had been woken several times by the same nightmare: one of the gigantic Finland ferries down by the quayside at Stadsgården crashed straight into the wall of Katarinaberget, which dropped steeply down to the water where the district of Södermalm brutally ended. The ferry was on its way into the city after crossing the Baltic, but instead of slowing down it seemed to be moving faster as it entered Saltsjön, then veered sharply to one side and headed straight for the wall at full speed. The violent impact sent a shock wave through the whole area, and made her apartment shudder. A second later she heard the sound of concrete and cement cracking along its seams, exposing the iron reinforcing bars and gradually succumbing to the shaking deep underground. It happened slowly, but before she could work out exactly what was going on, her apartment broke away from the rest of the building, toppled forward and crashed down onto the street.

She usually woke up halfway through the fall, just as she realized she was going to die.

It was always hard to get back to sleep afterward, with her heart pounding and her head spinning. Sometimes she got up and stood by the living room window with a glass of water, gazing out as if to reassure herself that everything was fine. The streetlamps glowed orange, and the headlights of the occasional cab sliced through the compact darkness of the late summer night.

Sometimes she stayed in bed, imagining the consequences of the disaster. First there would be the news bulletins, breathless reporters down at the port where the ferry lay on its side, its bow crushed; a chaotic flurry of helicopters, ambulances and small boats fishing people out of the water. "Do we have any idea how many casualties there might be?" the news anchor asked; the reporter on the spot said they didn't have any information yet, but they were expecting a significant toll. "How did it happen?" "No one knows." There was wild speculation on social media, and in a Flashback Forum thread that was updated several times a minute, a number of contributors suggested it must be a terrorist attack. Someone must have forced the captain to sail the ferry at speed into the wall. Maybe the real target was the Old Town, but he had managed to change course at the last second. Just imagine, one person wrote, if the ferry had crashed into the Old Town at that speed. The buildings would have fallen like dominoes.

Then her fantasy took her high above Östra Söder, giving her a bird's-eye view. Her apartment wasn't the only thing that had fallen down. The bunkers, traffic tunnels and subway tunnels that had been blasted out of the rock had caused the whole structure to give way; enormous sinkholes had appeared, and an entire section had completely collapsed. She often thought that Stockholm must be full of holes, like a Swiss cheese, with all its tunnels and passageways, and now the ferry disaster had shattered something deep in the very heart of the city.

She pictured the new subway station after the impact. The columns would have snapped in half, the fresco-covered ceiling would have crashed to the ground. Like the Acropolis. In her imagination it almost looked right, as if that had been the intention from the start. Sooner or later all buildings crumble, as does everything on this earth, it's the law of nature. The universe reduces everything to sand and dust, ground down by time. Classicism was the style best suited to ruins. Albert Speer had realized exactly that when he visited Rome and saw the ruins of the buildings that were the legacy of the Roman emperors. This had led him to ban the use of concrete and iron reinforcements in the grandest Nazi construction projects, because marble and brick made for more beautiful ruins. It is through the interpretation of ruins that we understand past civilizations—Speer knew that. If we are building for eternity, we must choose materials worthy of the task.

In an antiquarian bookshop a few years ago she had bought a book with the depressing title *The Destruction of Europe's Artworks*. It had been published in 1949, and contained hundreds of photographs of buildings that had been destroyed during the Second World War: French and Italian cathedrals and palaces, frescoes and fountains, central European inner cities with rows of houses, squares and bridges. "This is a cavalcade of images for all those who want to remember what they once saw while traveling around Europe, and for all those who never had the opportunity to see what is now gone forever," said the blurb on the back cover. "It is a monument to the splendor and greatness of Western civilization."

The final sentence made her shudder, partly because it was so chillingly beautiful, and partly because it was this very dream of the splendor and greatness of Western civilization that had led to the devastation of the accumulated beauty contained within the pages of the book. Before and after pictures showed the Malatesta Temple in Rimini, with only the Roman arches remaining in the later image, steadfastly bearing nothing but air; the Église Saint Germain in Argentan in Normandy, collapsed like a half-eaten gingerbread house; the magnificent royal palace in Budapest, with its shattered dome exposing a skeleton of beams, and in the foreground the impressive Chain Bridge across the Danube, sunken and half-drowned in the river. And then there was the Frauenkirche in Dresden, little more than a heap of bricks and pulverized mortar. The temperature inside had reached one thousand degrees during the Allied bombing raid, the pillars had glowed red-hot, and then the intense heat had caused them to explode, bringing down the enormous Baroque church.

She hadn't seen any of these buildings or visited any of the towns and cities in which they were located, but she felt as if she had. She felt like a part of something greater as she leafed through the book, a part of the civilization that had created those Renaissance frescoes and basilicas, Gothic cathedrals, city life, democracy, beautiful places in which to live.

Every time she tried to get back to sleep after the nightmare about the ferry disaster, and sometimes for days afterward, she was haunted by the thought of death and destruction. Her ageing, childless body, death creeping inexorably closer, a feeling of resignation, a suspicion that if she did meet a man now, right at the last minute, who wanted to try to impregnate her, it would probably fail, for reasons that she didn't know but almost certainly existed, physical defects that would come to light, the hidden diseases that the tabloid headlines were always shouting about; she would turn out to be carrying several of these diseases, having nurtured them in her body for decades.

She had never been pregnant, although she had thought she was on a number of occasions. Once she had been almost convinced, in the early days with Karl Johan, when they had had sex without using protection one night when they were drunk. She had checked her diary the next day and realized there was a risk she could have conceived, or a chance—she had never thought of it that way before, but the knowledge that it could actually happen, within the most serious relationship she had ever had, made her feel hopeful rather than panic-stricken.

A few days later she had felt odd, slightly nauseous, and she had lost her appetite. She googled the signs of early pregnancy and read that it was much too soon to have any symptoms at all, but in a discussion forum many women claimed to have experienced changes from the very first moment of conception. Several referred to nausea and a lack of appetite. Within hours she began to feel tired, a heavy, implacable weariness that meant she had to go to bed for a nap in the middle of the afternoon, she could hardly keep her eyes open. When she woke up she googled "tiredness": again, several women had experienced exactly the same thing as an early sign of pregnancy, and described that same irresistible exhaustion. A day or so later she thought she might be getting a cold, so she googled that too. A general feeling of not being very well, like an approaching cold—yes, that was another common early sign.

She didn't say anything to Karl Johan, for reasons she couldn't explain, but she kind of enjoyed having a secret, even if she didn't know whether she really did have a secret; it was much too early to do a test. The awareness of a "maybe" was indescribably satisfying, utterly absorbing. She looked at herself in the mirror and thought she had something of the glow that pregnant women are supposed to have, as if there were a light inside her shining through her eyes. Her face looked soft and gentle, almost holy.

She had never really thought about children up to that point, and she and Karl Johan had discussed it only as an abstract idea, something to consider in the distant future. Suddenly, however, she knew that if she did turn out to be pregnant, it would be wonderful. She began to regard the women she met in the city in a different way; she was part of a new, unspoken community, filled with a kind of biological happiness she had never known before or since, which united her with women throughout the history of the world: they shared the same power, the same secret.

Then her period had arrived bang on time a couple of weeks later; it was almost as if her body wanted to tell her that she had been stupid to imagine anything else. Even though it was a relief on a purely practical level, because it might not have been the right time for a baby just then, the disappointment when she saw the bloodstains on her panties was immeasurably greater.

What would she be remembered for? She might end up with neither children nor a partner; what had she done to make an impression on the world? Her writing didn't interest many people. Maybe she ought to write more, something really radical. Surely she ought to express her opinion when she had one, for example in the debate on the columns in the new subway station? If everything else was doomed to disappear into oblivion, the least she could do was to write what she really thought.

With a surge of determination, she picked up her phone.

. . .

Hans Jerup preferred to call his writers when he wanted something, which Karolina found incredibly frustrating. He was always perfectly charming when she spoke to him, but she loathed using the phone; it always made her feel as if she'd been found out, irrespective of what she was doing when it rang. She hoped the whole phone thing would soon die out, defeated in the evolution of technology by a medium more suited to the new generations who had grown up with the more sympathetic habit of communicating with the rest of the world in writing.

She sent him a text: "Hi Hans! Do you have time for lunch one day soon? I'd like to talk about contributing more. Karolina A."

She pressed "send" and received a reply in less than a minute.

"Karolina—is that really what you're thinking about on a Saturday night?"

She stared at the message.

It was a bold response, and yet her first instinct was embarrassment. It hadn't even occurred to her that it was Saturday. It was almost eight thirty. People with lives are busy doing things right now, she thought, and immediately remembered that when she was a teenager and hardly had any friends, she had always been afraid that someone would ask her what she had done at the weekend (read), or, worst of all, on the first day back in school after holidays which should have involved parties— Walpurgis Night or Lucia—and that same question again (read, probably).

I'm an adult now, she thought. I don't have to explain myself. And what kind of answer is that from an editor; what's with the sly, condescending tone? Or is it an invitation at the same time?

"Obviously." she replied, making a point of including the period. It made the single word look even shorter and more decisive. What the hell was Jerup up to anyway? If you're doing something enjoyable on a Saturday night, you don't answer work texts within sixty seconds.

Her cell immediately pinged again: "Sorry. I just assumed someone like you would be doing exciting things in the evenings. Of course I'd like to meet for lunch."

Someone like me? She hadn't even begun to formulate a response when the next message arrived:

"By the way, don't you live in Söder?"

"I do."

"I'm sitting in a bar in Nytorget. My companion had to leave. Why don't you come over? It would be more fun than lunch—I'll buy you a drink."

Is this normal? she thought. Is this normal in Denmark? Going out on a Saturday night for a drink with your boss—is that the famous relaxed, spontaneous Danish approach to life? Then she realized she didn't care; it was Saturday and she was single and what was she doing? Nothing, as usual.

"Okay—I'll be there in half an hour."

She had refreshed her makeup and changed into a dress. On the way to Nytorget she glanced at her reflection in a shop window. She liked the way she looked tonight, liked the fact that she gave the impression of being carefree, at ease with herself: high heels, trench coat flapping, hair caught up in a casual topknot. She thought the woman in the reflection seemed like a woman who did things on impulse. That was as far from her true nature as it was possible to get, and the whole situation gave her a sense of unreality, as if she were appearing in a film. Tonight she was playing the woman who cheerfully goes off to meet the arts editor for a drink.

She spotted him from some distance away; he was sitting by the counter that ran along the big window overlooking the square. A few years ago it had been a very hip place; now it was kind of passé, but in a way that appealed to her. These days only people who lacked the killer instinct for which places were really in dared to go there; the trendy crowd had moved on, like a swarm of locusts looking for a new area to colonize. She found the fact that he had chosen this bar quite touching, as if he were just any middle-aged man with a reasonable idea of what was cool.

When he took over as arts editor a few years earlier he had been more or less demonized in the press, and across the political spectrum concerns had been expressed—should we really be importing the Danish attitude to debate into Sweden? In six months Jerup had injected new life into the paper's arts pages and made them the most talked-about in the country. He had achieved this with a mixture of competent, well-written reviews and committed discussion, and had made a huge effort to bring in fresh voices rather than just the same old gang. He had appeared on panels and on sofas on daytime TV, joined in with studio debates, turned up on the radio station P1 in the afternoons, and had come across as an unusual combination of the cheerful and the combative. He always made a positive impression and quickly became popular, in spite of the fact that he represented a culturally conservative position that most people would have assumed—and hoped—would be out of step with the ethos of the times. Soon he was being referred to as a breath of fresh air.

Karolina had liked him from the start, and she liked him in the bar in Nytorget too. He radiated an energy that was rare in Stockholm's cultural circles, a man who was hungry for life, somehow slightly unkempt, with thinning hair and more than the hint of a belly, but he had a fire in his eyes—she didn't know how else to describe it—that made him extremely attractive.

"Welcome to Kongens Nytorv!" he said heartily as he greeted her with a hug. She wondered if he had spent a long time thinking up his opening gambit; if so, it was quite sweet that he had made the effort. Although maybe it wasn't new; maybe he had greeted the companion he had mentioned in his text message in exactly the same way. She wondered if it had been a male or female companion.

"What would you like to drink?" he asked when she had sat down beside him.

"Wine, please."

He picked up a menu from the counter, found the wine list and handed it to her.

"They have a good Barbera," he said.

She had no idea what a Barbera was. "Is that what you're drinking?"

He nodded. The wine list was divided into two sections, but rather than red and white, it was wines from the old and new worlds.

"Have you seen this?" she said. "The old and the new world. Fantastic."

"It might look fantastic, but is it really the right way to present a wine list?"

He was smiling as he challenged her.

"You mean it's Eurocentric?"

"Absolutely. It upholds a colonial point of view. Of course the new world has never been new in the objective sense, and even for us Europeans it hasn't been new since the end of the fifteenth century."

"That gives you something to rant about in your column on Sunday."

He laughed. The waiter appeared, a young man in tight jeans and a white T-shirt; Karolina asked for a glass of Burgundy, and he brought it right away.

"The old world," Jerup said, nodding at her glass.

"I like the old world."

"Cheers to the old world."

"And old values?"

"Definitely."

He laughed again; he always seemed to be in a good mood. She wondered what it was like to be that kind of person. She lowered her eyes, scanned his hands for a fraction of a second, looking for a ring. It was a routine check and she had mastered it perfectly; the glance was no more than a blink. He wasn't wearing a ring.

"That business of the old and new worlds is only a description," she said. "Not an evaluation."

He nodded. "And even if it were an evaluation," he said, "surely the general perception is that new is better than old? That's why the residents of this city will soon have ripped out and replaced every single kitchen in Stockholm."

"Exactly. New is better than old."

"Except when it comes to money, perhaps? Old money."

"As long as the money pays for kitchen renovations, I'm not sure it really matters."

It was a totally meaningless conversation, and she thought it was wonderful. She wanted to sink down into it as if it were a bath with the water at the perfect temperature, or a really soft bed, and never have to come back to reality. It was such a long time since she had had that kind of conversation with someone.

"I think the new world sounds good," she went on. "After all, it means that's the world that has the future to look forward to."

"You're right. We'll be sitting here in our old Europe, being overtaken by one continent after another."

"But everything is cyclical, like the seasons. Or stylistic trends. It's the fall here now, evening, Mannerism. But one day the spring will come again. Hopefully."

He looked searchingly at her; she could see that he understood what she was talking about.

"The spring will always come again," he said.

It sounded so reassuring. He ordered more wine for both of them, then started telling her a story about one of the other writers on the paper, a reasonably well-known author, then the narrative wound its way elegantly into the literary world in general, where they spent some time discussing a critic with one of the other daily papers, both agreeing that they disliked him a great deal. Karolina laughed out loud at Hans's character assassination of the guy.

Suddenly the main overhead lights came on and she blinked at the sudden brightness, irritated that someone had accidentally switched them on. Then she realized the bar was closing. She checked the display on her cell phone; it was much later than she would have guessed.

"So..." she said.

"So," Hans repeated with a hint of resignation. He said it again when they had slowly and slightly clumsily gathered up their things, put on their coats and found themselves standing outside in a light but persistent drizzle, almost as if the night air were suffused with dampness, making the streetlamps look as if they had been painted in watercolors that were too wet, each surrounded by a fuzzy halo. It was mild, a pleasant early autumn evening. People were wandering around the square, several places had closed at the same time, and a line was forming outside a bar that was still open.

"Do you want to go over there?" Jerup asked.

"I hate standing in line."

He smiled, fished a packet of cigarettes out of his coat pocket and lit up as he looked at her, watching and waiting. She thought about her dream of the ferry disaster, about the ruins and Mannerism, about the autumn of everything. A few years ago she had read a list on some click site, allegedly based on interviews with those involved in palliative care. It had ranked the things people regretted most on their deathbed. Not having had more sex was top of the list.

"Maybe you'd like to come back to my place?" she suggested.

"Sure."

She stole a glance at their reflections in the same shop window on the way to her apartment. Her hair had dropped a little thanks to the damp air, but it didn't really matter; she still liked what she saw. Jerup was by her side, tall and well-dressed, chatting away happily and making her laugh. She thought they could be taken for a couple. A good-looking couple, newly in love. She wanted someone to see them and think exactly that. She had a strong feeling that she could be part of a couple with him. He would be good for her; he was intelligent but uncomplicated, which was both unusual and attractive.

Things happened fast when they got through the door. She went into the kitchen to open a bottle of wine, but she had only just gotten the glasses out when he came and stood behind her and placed his hand on her waist. She turned around, he kissed her, and she clung to him with an intensity that surprised him for a moment, she could tell, but then he obviously decided he liked it and lifted her onto the kitchen counter and started clumsily unbuttoning her dress.

It was all a little clumsy in bed too, they were both drunk, but it was still good, maybe even wonderful, wonderful to feel the weight of his body on hers, and wonderful afterward when he drew her close and they quickly fell asleep, then it was light outside when she looked at him again, he was snoring, he seemed to be in a deep sleep.

Her brain was woolly from the wine. Hans Jerup still smelled good the morning after the night before, and he still looked good in the unforgiving daylight. He came into the kitchen, half-dressed and with tousled hair, as Karolina was flicking through the newspapers and waiting for the coffee to brew. He poured himself a glass of juice and gulped it down, then kissed the top of her head in passing before he picked up *Svenska Dagbladet*, turned to the arts section and gave it his full attention.

"I guess I'd better make a move," he said after he had drunk the cup of coffee she had given him, and they had chatted for a while about the contents of the papers in a way that was so enjoyable, much more enjoyable than breakfast with Karl Johan had ever been. "I have to prepare for a debate at the Cultural Center:

the challenges of journalism in the digital age. The most boring topic in the world, plus we've been talking about it for how long? Ten years? Fifteen?"

He sighed, but still looked pleased.

"Where do you live?" she asked.

"Kungsholmen. The paper owns an apartment that I'm using, but I still have my own apartment in Copenhagen; I spend most weekends there."

"I'd do the same."

He cleared his throat. "My girlfriend lives there too. Or whatever you call it at my age. Partner. But I don't really like that word."

Partner. Of course. Had she really imagined that a man like Hans Jerup would be available? To someone like her? Stupid. How stupid she was.

"Who is she?"

"She's an actress—Tove Winther. But she's not especially well-known in Sweden."

Perhaps the last comment was meant to offer some kind of consolation, but it didn't work. Karolina knew exactly who Tove Winther was. She could see her in her mind's eye, pictured in a fashion magazine when she had the lead role in a Swedish TV series a few years earlier. She was very beautiful, with long, flowing blonde hair. And young—was she even thirty? Of course Hans Jerup was with someone like her. Someone completely unattainable.

I have to stop falling for everyone, she thought when he had gone. He had given her a warm hug, making her wish that it would never end, and that he would decide to spend this terrible sunny Sunday with her, and that there was no girlfriend in Copenhagen.

After her relationship with Anders had faded away, she had often thought about Eleanor of Aquitaine, the twelfth-century French queen who had established a "court of love." She had read about it when she was a teenager, and the story had appealed to her obsession with justice and fairness. As an adult, of course, she understood that emotional fairness was a contradiction in itself, something that could never exist in reality except in a form that wouldn't make anyone happy. But still. Wouldn't it have been fairer, she often thought, if Anders had been married to her, someone with whom he would have had a fantastic life, rather than to a woman with whom life was just about tolerable? And wouldn't it be fairer if she was Hans Jerup's girlfriend, rather than Tove Winther? Anyway, what did he talk to his girlfriend about when he was in Copenhagen? Didn't Karolina deserve him more?

This last thought was embarrassing, because she knew perfectly well that love isn't something we deserve or earn, it's not an account where we can overdraw, then expect someone to make a deposit so we're back in the black. She even found such comments irritating when she came across them on social media, motivational quotes such as "You deserve to be happy, honey!" Deserve, she would think; it doesn't work like that. Unfortunately it doesn't work like that.

She had mentoring sessions with two students the following day. The first was Olof Bodin, whose name always made her picture an elderly gentleman, but Olof was around thirty, tall and slim, screwing up his eyes as he peered through his glasses. He was the editor of *Notos*, an arts journal that hadn't created much of a stir, but usually attracted a modicum of attention when a new edition was published and the daily papers needed a paragraph or two. She knew two young female poets helped out with the editing. From the very first time they met, Olof had made it clear that she had a standing invitation to get involved in *Notos*, which she had yet to take up. However, she liked to hear him talk about his work on the journal, because he always did so with an enthusiasm that he seemed to expect her to share, and she found that touching.

Olof was undertaking a reception study of Jim Månsson, the Swedish postmodernist who was both acclaimed and beloved during the 1980s. He had died of an overdose and was now regarded as something of a genius who had passed away far too young. The initial proposal had focused on romantic tendencies in Månsson's work, which was presumably why Olof had been allocated to her, but he had soon changed his mind, citing a lack of a solid base on which to build, and instead had decided on a basic reception study, which was one of the most boring things Karolina could imagine.

She realized he was saying something about Žižek; she had lost concentration completely. Then she grasped that he was actually talking about a piece he was working on for *Notos*. He looked pleased as he explained that it was going to be a themed issue on psychoanalysis.

"Cool," she murmured, although she knew perfectly well that it was the wrong word, because *Notos* wasn't supposed to be cool.

Olof Bodin was the perfect representative of an attitude that was becoming increasingly common, in her opinion: undergraduate and postgraduate students who treated theories as truths rather than theories, and who found theories about art more interesting than the art itself. Which annoyed her. If she had had any say, her subject would still have been called the history of art, and she would have insisted that everyone who set foot in the department produce an essay in which they wrote in detail about a historical work of their choice, explaining exactly why they thought it was interesting or good or significant, or poor and overrated for that matter, anything, just as long as they expressed some kind of feeling for the work itself and not just the theories surrounding it.

"*Con amore!*" one of the professors who had taught the foundation course when she was a student had impressed upon them: with love, from the heart, that was the best basis for research, just as it was for anyone contemplating marriage.

"So what do you think of Jim Månsson?" she said abruptly.

Olof looked somewhat taken aback.

"Well, he's one of the foremost representatives of Swedish postmodernism."

"Yes. He is. But that's a fact. Why are you interested in him? What is it that's made you choose to devote several years of your life to him in particular?"

"I think he says something relevant about the time in which he lived."

"What does he say?"

Olof's eyes were darting all over the place. It was hardly surprising that his journal was the equivalent of a sleeping pill. Then he cleared his throat.

"There's a fragility about him," he began. "That might not be the right word, but there's an element in the evasiveness in his paintings that doesn't seem studied or cynical, it's...it's as if it reflects an actual experience. You might not see it at first, because his painting often has such powerful expression, but the woman turning away in *Breakfast on Ringgatan*, for example... There is almost something reminiscent of Whistler about her. A kind of melancholy ease. I think Månsson has the ability to depict deeply felt emotions in a form that is..."

He fell silent, searching for the right word; he waved his hand vaguely in the air as if he were trying to catch it.

"...shimmering."

Karolina smiled at him. It was beautifully put, and Olof had also managed to capture an aspect of Månsson she had never thought of before, which would make her look at his paintings with fresh interest. She told Olof exactly that, and he looked both embarrassed and delighted at the same time.

"Maybe you should write an article about this instead?" she suggested, but he shuffled uncomfortably.

"The thing is, I've spent hours reading Žižek," he mumbled.

She still felt lighthearted, filled with a hope that had been absent for a long time. She tended to have low expectations of most people, not least her students. Maybe she was too hard on them. Maybe they had hidden depths, if she just dug below the surface.

She just managed to grab another coffee before it was time for Anton Strömberg's session. He arrived with rosy cheeks, tousled hair and sparkling eyes, clutching a large envelope.

"Wait till you see this!" he said excitedly, as if she were a child at a circus about to witness the most amazing feats, and she almost felt that way as he drew out a bundle of papers.

"I've printed everything I photographed," he went on. "This is a small part of Ebba Ellis's graphics."

He handed her the papers. The first picture was an etching with decisive yet sensitive lines showing a proud Penelope sitting on a cliff by the sea with a shuttle in her hand. She was as power-fully drawn as Ebba's Salome had been in *Ord & Bild*, solid, with a weight that reminded Karolina of Michelangelo.

The next image showed Echo and Narcissus, the nymph cup-ping her hands around her mouth and calling vainly to the youth who couldn't tear his eyes away from his own reflection in the small pool separating them.

"Sad," Anton commented.

Karolina smiled. "Yes—there's a woman who's going to be unhappy."

"I think she'll soon realize she's too good for him," Anton said. "She'll be fine—you can see she's strong."

He was right—you could see that she was strong. Just like Penelope, waiting for Odysseus. Not to mention Salome, who appeared later in the bundle. She really did look like a woman who could demand a man's head on a platter without even blinking.

They were all good pictures; Karolina would have thought the same even if they hadn't fit so perfectly into her own field. Definitely a valuable addition to Swedish art history, produced by an artist who was clearly a skilled technician, and with an inter-national orientation. And she was a woman, ignored by history. Exciting.

"Very interesting," she said to Anton, who was looking expec-tantly at her. "You've made quite a find."

He smiled. "You haven't seen the best yet."

He passed her several more sheets of paper: grainy, barely legi-ble copies of letters that had been photographed in poor light. The handwriting was old-fashioned, the language German. "Lieber Franz," the first one began; after that she could make out only the odd word. It was signed "deine Ebba."

"What's this?"

"Look at the next one."

She sighed, annoyed at having to let him call the shots. The next page was another blurred copy of a letter, with half the page taken up by a sketch of a naked woman, leaning back slightly, with a thick black snake coiled around her body. Across her thighs, between them, around her back, its head resting on her shoulder, leering at the observer.

"Is it Stuck?" Karolina asked.

The German symbolist Franz von Stuck's most famous paintings were of women with snakes in a variety of compositions that were all more or less identical to the picture in front of her. There was a late, slightly less indecent version in the Alte Nationalgalerie in Berlin in a magnificent gold frame. These paintings were some of her absolute favorites when it came to German Symbolism: the woman was Eve, who had given in to temptation and wasn't ashamed. Totally different from the Renaissance, where Eve was often utterly crushed by what she had done—Masaccio's Eve in *Expulsion from the Garden of Eden*, for example, sobbing as she desperately and clumsily tries to hide her sinful body. Stuck had painted a woman who was not ashamed of her sexuality—quite the reverse.

She was going to say that to Anton, but changed her mind. It might embarrass him.

"That's one of my favorite paintings," she said instead.

"That's by Ebba Ellis," Anton informed her.

"Right—so she did the sketch based on Stuck?"

"No—check out the date."

The letter was neatly dated March 1888. It meant nothing to her. She was starting to lose patience again.

"1888—so?"

"Stuck didn't paint his first woman with a snake until 1889," Anton said. "Which means I have reason to believe that this is what gave him the idea. Ebba Ellis sends him this drawing, which he later uses, with her permission, as the basis for his most famous paintings. He has Ebba to thank for everything."

Karolina examined the sketch. It was so similar to Stuck's famous work that there could be no doubt they were linked.

"Are you sure?"

Anton smiled. "How cool is that?"

"Where the hell did you get ahold of this?"

He leaned back in his chair, looking smug. "I spent some time working for an auction house in Malmö. I don't know if you're familiar with that kind of thing…"

His tone was supercilious, as if he presumed she knew nothing about it. Perhaps it wasn't surprising; most of those involved in the theory and history of art probably thought the world of auction houses was vulgar, and he assumed she was one of them. Maybe she was, but she had lived with Karl Johan, who had cheerfully thrown himself into the whole thing and didn't hesitate to play along with the vulgarity.

"Very familiar," she said.

Anton looked crestfallen, as if she had ruined the beginning of a story he had carefully planned.

"As I told you before, I was contacted by a relative of Ebba Ellis," he said after clearing his throat. "He owns most of the art she produced, although the odd drawing turns up at auction occasionally. However, she sold very little while she was alive, so there isn't much on the market. That means his collection isn't worth a great deal, unfortunately, because however good she was, people just aren't prepared to pay big money for someone who's completely unknown. But I was curious, so I started looking into her background. Her relative knew which schools she'd attended in Germany, and that she'd spent a lot of time in Munich, but that was about as far as I got. Then I mentioned it to my boss, who tipped me off about an art dealership in Berlin—Dernburgs. Do you know it?"

"No."

"It's run by Max Dernburg, who is one of Germany's leading experts in symbolic art. A wonderful man. Well-dressed, polite, educated. Discreet. I'm sure he has amazing stories to tell if you really get to know him, but you have no idea how discreet gentlemen of that generation can be. I'd rather entrust my secrets to him than my therapist. He was very familiar with Ebba Ellis's work, and had even sold one of her drawings—*Odysseus and Circe*. It's a decent effort, but not her best."

Karolina could picture Dernburgs art dealership, with Max Dernburg dressed in a tweed jacket, perhaps surrounded by the aroma of pipe tobacco, his pleasant, low-key manner hiding a skilled businessman and a knowledgeable dealer.

"I visited him several times before he agreed to help me, but the good thing about educated people is that you can gain their respect if you really have something to offer. The second time I saw him, he said no one had ever asked him about Ellis. And the third time he gave me the name of a woman he thought would know more: Lotte Baumann."

He paused briefly, as if to allow the name to sink in.

"She's the daughter of Elsie Baumann, who was Stuck's mistress. She's over eighty, at a guess, maybe nearer ninety, but as sharp as you or me. She never said it straight out, but I actually think she could be Franz von Stuck's daughter. He left a considerable amount of money to her mother, which then came to Lotte. And not just money—she owns several paintings by him. She also has his letters. You should see her apartment. I don't even think it's possible to live like that in Stockholm. It's on the top floor of a fantastic old building on a side street off Fasanenstraße, with huge arched windows, lots of art, a wonderful library, big palms, the most stunning view... It's as if time has stood still in there for the last hundred years."

"And she just let you in?"

"My German is very good," he said with a smile. "And it was just the same as with Dernburg: Ebba Ellis's name got me in. I can't deny that she seemed to enjoy the company of a young man..."

He smiled again.

"...but I think she really liked the idea of passing on the information in those letters to someone who was genuinely interested. She might not have many years left; I'm probably her last chance."

He reached for the pile of photographed letters.

"There's some excellent stuff in here. Stuck and Ebba Ellis seem to have had a fascinating relationship. I don't think it was romantic; they were simply friends, very close friends. Soul mates, almost. They were in regular contact, they saw each other often and discussed everything that was going on around them, especially in the art world. He treated her as his intellectual equal. At the same time, I think you can read something between the lines now and again, a slightly charged atmosphere, a hint of jealousy on her part when another woman is mentioned, a warmth between them which is very touching."

"You could be right," Karolina said. "It could well be that the best relationships are those that never become romantic, or sexual, but have the potential to develop that way. There's a kind of suppressed attraction that is never talked about or allowed to emerge, and it heightens the whole relationship."

He looked her straight in the eye.

"Yes..." he began, then he seemed to lose the thread and lowered his gaze.

The atmosphere in the room suddenly felt highly charged. Karolina cleared her throat.

"This is very interesting, Anton. It's an entirely new direction in Swedish art history. I know there was contact between Prince Eugen and Arnold Böcklin, for example, but I think that was mostly concerned with practical matters. I think I've seen an invitation asking Böcklin if he'd like to exhibit in Stockholm, for example. This is something completely different, such an extensive intellectual and artistic exchange between a Swedish artist and German Symbolism. I would say that this will make Ebba Ellis stand out as the only real exponent of an internationally orientated Symbolism in Sweden."

This time Anton's smile was positively enchanting. She wanted to see him smile like that more often, she thought; it made her smile right back at him.

"For real?" he said, his voice a little unsteady. She nodded, realizing that she just couldn't stop smiling. She probably ought to calm down rather than getting him all fired up. She wanted to tell him not to mention the subject to anyone, especially not the collection of letters in Berlin. Not until his dissertation had been completed and accepted, and was ready to face the world.

"Have you told Lennart about this?" she burst out. "About the letters?"

He shook his head. "I didn't get that far. I guess Lennart Olsson is his favorite topic of conversation."

Karolina laughed, and the expression on his face was happy, relieved; it felt as if she looked right into him and saw herself. It was a sense of the deepest companionship, combined with gratitude at being a part of what he had discovered. It was all so moving, the fact that a hotel cleaner's son was responsible for such a scoop, and had a brilliant, well-deserved academic career to look forward to. It was fair. At last something in life was fair.

She wanted to kiss him. It was a crazy impulse, she knew that as soon as the moment had passed, but for a second she thought they were alike, and it was an overwhelming feeling.

When he had left her office she sat back in her chair. This was wonderful. Anton's dissertation could well be the most talked about for many years. It couldn't be better: not only had he found a forgotten female artist, but she was a woman who had pushed the boundaries in the time in which she lived, she was independent, unafraid, creative. The link to Germany and the contact with Stuck were the icing on the cake. An unknown Swedish artist had actually been behind his famous snake women. That would send reverberations right through the world in which Karolina worked.

She could see it now, an exhibition introducing Ebba Ellis's work, her exchange with Franz von Stuck and all those links to the German symbolist movement. It could be staged in collaboration with a German gallery, perhaps the magnificent Villa Stuck in Munich, which she had always wanted to visit. Not only did the contemporary scene love forgotten women, it would also be possible to show how perfectly suited to the twenty-first century Ellis's motifs were. This was a discovery that would bring into the limelight the epoch Karolina had focused on during her time at the university. Both she and Anton would be able to write for the expensive catalogue that would accompany the exhibition. She pictured the private viewing, she and Anton standing side by side in a beautiful gallery in Munich, each holding a glass of sparkling wine, laughing, so happy. It would give her status within the department, she saw rows of jealous colleagues before her. Ebba Ellis's life story was something quite different from Lennart Olsson's depressing epigones of female modernists. He had described Anton's topic as "so interesting" in spite of the fact that he knew only that Ellis had existed; Karolina tried to imagine his reaction when he heard about the rest, the contact and the correspondence with Stuck, the sketch of the woman with the snake. He would be green with envy.

She also imagined Anton's dissertation, possibly published by one of the more prestigious houses that rarely dealt with that kind of book, but on this occasion they would make an exception, they would realize that this was something they couldn't turn down, that the material was bound to attract international interest. It would be a beautiful book, richly illustrated, tastefully designed. And on the title page there would be a dedication: "Warm thanks to Karolina Andersson. Without your support and encouragement, Ebba Ellis would still be unknown to the world." Which would be perfectly true. Through her guidance she would help to add a vital piece to the jigsaw puzzle of art history.

And even though Anton would be at the center of it all, she would experience the success through him. She thought that seemed fair too.

. . .

At the weekend she rented a car and went to visit her parents. She rarely drove; Karl Johan had always been the driver if they were going somewhere, but as she left the city after picking up a red Toyota Yaris from the underground parking lot at Slussen, she felt both independent and lighthearted. She couldn't remember the last time she had felt that way.

The traffic was heavy at first, even though she thought she had set off before most people finished work. She clearly wasn't the only one with that intention. She virtually came to a standstill on the E4 just outside Södertälje, then suddenly things started moving again. It was a warm, sunny autumn afternoon, the leaves had just begun to turn yellow and she put the music on nice and loud, a playlist with songs she liked from the eighties. She had been too young to appreciate the decade at the time, but had learned to love it retrospectively. Karl Johan had had no interest whatsoever in pop music, and had insisted on listening to classical and contemporary music on the radio station P2 during their outings. That had been okay; it was worse when he decided to listen to a CD called *Swedish Earrings*, with Zarah Leander singing "Do You Want to See a Star?" and Karl Gerhard's "Jazz Boy." It wasn't what she would have chosen, but if she was in a good mood it was quite pleasant, until Povel Ramel started singing something totally unbearable, and she just had to switch it off. She would have to bite her tongue to stop herself from kicking off an argument—how could Karl Johan possibly want to listen to Povel Ramel?—and when she glanced at him she would feel a shudder of revulsion. Surely if she really loved a man who loved Povel Ramel, she wouldn't feel disgusted by him? But she did.

She stopped at a gas station in Söderköping to buy coffee and a bar of chocolate. She called her parents and told them she would soon be there, then turned the music up even louder as she set off along the final stretch of the E22 heading south, reinvigorated by caffeine and sugar.

"Gusum Interchange," announced the Highways Agency's bottle green signs. The name was depressing in itself; she thought "Gusum" was an ugly word, both typographically and aurally. As she slowly drove through the small community, it occurred to her that it was exactly the right kind of name for this kind of place.

She passed the center, which consisted of little more than a grocery store and a pizzeria, and the sign that proclaimed "Almost the best water in Sweden," pointing to a small drinking fountain that she had never dared try, because she thought it looked extremely unhygienic. Someone had tried to cross out the word "almost" with a marker pen that didn't work properly, in order to give the impression that Gusum in fact had the very best water in Sweden.

Her parents lived in a house at the end of a road in one of the sparsely populated areas that made up the town. They were both retired now; her father had worked in sales at an electronics company and her mother had run a small family day care, like a number of other mothers in the locality. There had always been children in the house while Karolina was growing up; they had spent most of their time in the playroom in the basement. She remembered the peace and quiet when they had gone home for the day, the calm dinners by the glow of the kitchen lamp in a house where the tranquility suddenly seemed palpable.

Many of the children became her playmates. They would run around outdoors in the forest nearby, building dens, playing hide-and-seek or rounders in a field where sheep used to graze, probably back in the fifties before the housing development began to spread. Sometimes they would set off on an expedition to the water tower looming high on a hill among the pine trees, or through the dense undergrowth to a dilapidated summer cottage. The recollection still sent a shiver of excitement down her spine: rotting trees and sun-bleached curtains, overgrown tiger lilies and long, yellowed grass in the garden, a table and chairs that had been left outside through too many winters, a broken rotary clothes dryer, faded copies of *Hemmets Journal* and a few porn magazines discovered in an outhouse where the door had been left open, hearts in their mouths in case anyone came along, an adult who might chase them away. Or even worse—something horrible, something that had taken over the cottage. There was a persistent rumor that lights had been seen inside at night, in spite of the fact that no one had lived there for many years.

Her memories were filled with a sense of security and freedom at the same time, which still seemed to her to be the epitome of happiness: spring evenings when the streets were freshly swept, the sky bright and clear and full of promise, when a hedgehog who had just woken up rustled around among the leaves under someone's deck and was enticed out with a little bit of liver pâté, the air heavy with the scent of lilacs, spring almost imperceptibly changing into summer, those endless days, evenings when the gardens were filled with the smell of barbecues and newly mown grass, potentilla and dog rose, sandboxes and playhouses, fruit trees and kitchen gardens with rhubarb leaves that were big enough to use as umbrellas, as satellite dishes picking up signals from space on those summer nights.

For Karolina that all-encompassing happiness was indelibly linked to life in this residential part of town. It was a universe all of its own, with its own narrative: dads gathering on someone's drive if there was a problem with the car, standing there chatting all evening; moms dutifully turning up at an enthusiastic neighbor's recurring Tupperware parties, children's parties, midsummer celebrations at the local community center. She remembered the early midsummer mornings when the dew lingered on the grass, picking lupins and red clover and daisies and cornflowers to make garlands and decorate the maypole, drinking coffee with home-baked bread and cakes, selling raffle tickets for the local sports club, the chocolate wheel where she won ten bars of chocolate on one blissful midsummer's day.

Gusum was a former industrial town which used to have a thriving brass manufacturing industry going back to the seventeenth century. Zippers had been produced well into the twentieth century in the attractive brick building in the middle of the town, beside the river. And as if it wasn't enough that the foundry had been closed down at the beginning of the 1990s, meaning that the area's largest employer ceased to exist and Gusum became the latest in a series of Swedish towns left bobbing around on the waves of modern life like a buoy, cast adrift without the mooring that the industry had provided—it was also discovered that polluted wastewater had been released into the river for most of the twentieth century. Investigations showed that the levels of environmental toxins were high in berries, mushrooms and fish. The area around the factory was more or less dead; the ground was barren, the trees ominously bare. A small-scale Swedish Chernobyl, she often thought. She pictured a sign at the entrance to the town: "Abandon hope all ye who enter here." Cleaning up the river had been a costly and time-consuming exercise.

The large quantity of empty houses and apartments following the depopulation of Gusum meant that there was plenty of room to take in refugees. This had happened on such a large scale that it had even been discussed on the national news. After many initial problems, particularly in the ICA store and on the bus route between Norrköping and Gusum, where fare-dodging and late-night brawls became a growing problem, the town had found a new balance, and new kind of normality. Everyday life went on as before, with a tacit acceptance of how things had developed.

She thought about Gusum every time she read articles in the daily newspapers analyzing the situation in the country, always from a Stockholm perspective. She was grateful that she had access to the reality the town represented, yet at the same time frustrated because it was a world that was seldom depicted in the media. And although she would always feel the greatest loyalty toward the residents of the small community and the lives they led, she would never dream of actually living there.

She contemplated the people moving across the square, their business the same as those in Södermalm at this time on a Friday: wine and the ingredients for a cozy night in, even if the wine had to be ordered in advance and picked up from the ICA store, and the ingredients themselves were probably very different.

"Karro?" a voice beside her suddenly said.

She hardly reacted at first; no one had called her Karro for over twenty years. Then she turned around and saw a tall man in a dark blue, coarse-knit sweater, eyes narrowed as he peered at her. He looked familiar. It took her a few seconds to realize it was Robban. She couldn't remember his surname, Lundström or Lundberg or Lundgren, something like that. They had been in the same class at elementary and middle school, then bumped into each other at the bus stop or in the pizzeria at regular intervals after their everyday lives were separated by new schools. She hadn't seen him since she moved to Linköping after graduating. He looked all grown-up now, like a caricature of the mental image she had of him, sitting on a moped with an air of self-assurance that was irresistible as far as most girls in town were concerned. Word of his good looks had spread to Valdemarsvik via the yearbook, and in eighth grade he had a girlfriend there, Cecilia Söder, the prettiest girl in the school. This gave him an aura of worldliness that made him even more exciting.

There was something heavy about him now; he was powerfully built, not overweight but almost, although he looked as if he worked out. He towered over her, his smile suggesting friendly curiosity rather than total self-confidence.

"Robban," she said, smiling back at him. She wondered if he thought she looked old, but he seemed delighted to see her.

"So you live in Stockholm now?" he said, his voice rising at the end of the sentence to form a question, although it was obviously a statement. Maybe it was common knowledge around here, where everyone knew everyone else.

"I do."

"And you work at the university?"

"Yes, I...I'm a professor these days..." She rolled her eyes disarmingly, it even sounded odd to her: standing in the street in Gusum announcing that she was a professor. "It sounds so...old."

He grinned. "It makes me think of an old man. Not...not someone like you."

That might just be a compliment, she thought. His voice was calm, pleasant, his accent hadn't changed at all since junior high, and she liked that. She had hated the Östergötland accent when she was younger, and had made a real effort to get rid of hers as soon as she came into contact with people who spoke differently: the pure, almost metallic tones of Uppsala, or the strange Skåne tone in Lund. She had encountered both as soon as she set foot in the university.

"So what are you up to?"

"I work in Viken. For the town council. I'm an IT technician."

That wouldn't have been her guess. To be fair, she had no idea what she would have said, but it would definitely have been something less qualified than an IT technician with the council.

"Sounds good."

"It's okay. Jeez, it's great to see you!"

He seemed very sincere, and she was touched. They had never had a great deal to do with each other, but she had always liked him. There was something appealing about him even back then, in junior high.

"Are you still in touch with anyone from school?" she asked.

"Well, Ola and Jonte still live here, so I see them pretty often, and Jenny, and Anna and Jesper live in Viken... That's about it, though."

Karolina nodded in spite of the fact that the names meant nothing to her. There had been several Annas in school, and several Jennys too; she had no idea which he meant, and she didn't care enough to ask. She had no recollection of a Jonte.

"Do you have a family?"

"Two kids. Every other week." He smiled again. "How about you?"

"No, I... I'm single."

So embarrassing. Was that even the right thing to say when you were over forty? What else could you say? Alone? That sounded really sad. Maybe she should go with "recently separated," but that gave the separation too much significance, as if it defined her.

Karl Johan had come with her to Gusum a few times, not exactly reluctantly, but he obviously had no interest in the place. She pictured him in the ICA store, getting mad because there was no coriander, biting his tongue at her parents' house to stop himself from commenting on the décor, a pleasant and unassuming mixture of IKEA and inherited pieces. His parents' imposing home outside Uppsala was full of genuine antiques, of course. He had looked totally out of place in the little square outside the pizzeria, in his expensive, neatly pressed clothes. He had a permanent aura of cleanliness, as if he had just stepped out of the shower, clean and rosy with barely a trace of any kind of body odor. When she started the affair with Anders, she had found the fact that he sometimes smelled of sweat incredibly arousing.

Robban was nodding as he absorbed the information that she was single.

"I know what that's like," he said sympathetically.

"I separated at the beginning of the summer. I mean, we separated. Although it was my decision."

"Doesn't make it any easier," he said kindly.

There was something about the light, the low autumn sun, that made her feel dizzy, as if time and space had ceased to exist. As she looked at Robban it could just as easily have been 1993, they could have been in school, standing in the warm sunshine by the bike rack, with drifts of maple leaves and blackberry twigs getting caught in the wheels, and gravel and cigarette butts and spat-out chewing gum, and mopeds and whispers like a carpet of sound in the background as she waited for him to ask...ask anything, really, but a question was essential, a question that could keep their lives attached for a little while longer. He hadn't asked back then, but he did now.

"So what are you doing tonight?"

"I have to have dinner with my parents."

"How about tomorrow?"

They were both smiling again.

"Tomorrow I'm not doing anything."

"Would you like to go for a drink?"

"That would be great."

They went on an outing on Saturday, with Karolina in the backseat and her parents in the front, just like when she was a little girl. She had always loved going out in the car; the small talk, some kind of discussion program playing quietly on the radio, gazing out at the scenery passing by. They had coffee and sandwiches by the sea, where the archipelago began; it was still warm in the sun.

Twilight was falling by the time she set off to meet Robban; he lived not far from her parents. The ditch along the edge of the road where she grew up was filled with the modest flowers of her childhood, the ones that were never included in a bouquet: mugwort, yarrow, tansy, all with tough stems and strong, aromatic scents that impregnated the palms of your hands. She rubbed a clump of humble mugwort flowers between her fingers; they smelled of schnapps. She knew she was thinking of wormwood, the mugwort's better-known relative, which was used for spicing spirits and in the making of absinthe. They smelled very similar.

Les fleurs du mal. That wasn't why wormwood bore its Swedish name, *malört*; it was because it was supposed to protect clothes against moths, which were also called *mal* in Swedish. However, the connection still seemed logical. "And the name of the star was wormwood," as it said in the Book of Revelation. The star that fell from the sky and made the water so bitter that people died, poisoned. She wondered how many had died as a consequence of the toxins discharged into the river in Gusum, Sweden's Chernobyl. Her parents had long since given up picking mushrooms and berries in the forests around the old foundry; they always went off in the car with the aim of getting as far away as possible.

Robban lived in a small house that had belonged to an old lady when they were little; there was no trace of her now. The place had been completely refurbished, with pale wallpaper, a large leather sofa and a TV with a hi-tech sound system. The television was on low, showing a nature documentary; a cheetah was chasing its prey across the savanna. The living room was different in every way from the living rooms in which she spent time in Stockholm. There were no bookshelves, no designer furniture. But it was pleasant, in a slightly inept way. A display cabinet housed slightly more expensive glass and china—presents, no doubt, maybe going back to confirmation and graduation, engagement and significant birthdays, and of course the wedding. It was a touching cabinet.

Robban gave her a drink in a glass that had probably been on display. There was something sweet in it, possibly Cinzano Bianco with lemonade, decorated with half a slice of lemon. She had to make an effort not to knock the whole lot back in one; he had been very generous with the lemonade. When he took a sip, he realized the problem.

"Oh wow," he murmured. "That's not exactly a stiff drink, is it?"

She laughed and shook her head. He managed a little smile; maybe he was nervous. He got up and brought the bottle of Cinzano, then topped up their glasses.

"Better?"

"Much better."

He seemed to relax then, and it was fun to talk to him, she liked herself when she was talking to him. Just for a while it was as if she went back to being someone she had left behind a long time ago, out of a sense of self-preservation, but now it was okay to let that person out again. He had produced a bottle of red wine; somehow it was empty, and he fetched another.

They reminisced, talking about people they both knew; he briefly mentioned his divorce, which he still hadn't gotten over. His wife had met someone else ("a rich bastard with a big house, he owns a company that sells tiles, the kids say the whole god-damn place looks like a bathroom") and moved to Valdemarsvik. He obviously thought what she had done was unforgivable, and had to make an enormous effort not to sound bitter.

"So what happened with your relationship?" he asked.

"I realized I wasn't in love with him anymore, and maybe I never had been."

"Fuck. Were you together long?"

"Far too long."

"Have you started dating again?"

Karolina didn't know how to answer that. It had never occurred to her that she ought to start dating. He had asked the question as it were self-evident, as if dating were a practical detail, the next logical step when you were single, like signing on for unemployment benefits when you lost your job. Was that how people thought? Was that how they lived? Was that why they had grown-up lives with families and houses and display cabinets, and she had a noisy two-room apartment full of books and loneliness?

"To be honest, I've mainly focused on work," she said evasively. It was a straight lie; she had never felt more distracted at work than over the past few months. What was she actually doing? A project on apes. How meaningless was that? The idea of mentioning such a thing while sitting on Robban's sofa was just bizarre. Why wasn't she doing something important? Something that counted in the real world?

"Do you enjoy it?" he wondered.

"Do I enjoy it...I suppose it's what I'm good at. And by this stage I've put so much time and energy into it that I can't stop. But I am looking forward to supervising a PhD student who's researching a completely unknown female symbolist—it's actually something of a scoop. The kind of thing you dream of."

"Wow," he said politely. "That's great. You deserve a bit of luck."

"There's a really important link to Germany, a whole series of letters between her and one of the most famous German artists of the period."

She fell silent when she saw from his face that he had absolutely no interest in what she was saying. On TV a talent show was reaching its climax, the audience was yelling; he looked at her, then leaned across and kissed her, a little tentatively. Maybe because he didn't know what else to do. The reason wasn't important, it was fun. They should have kissed years ago. They fell back on the sofa as one, she closed her eyes and thought how wonderful it was to feel his weight on her, wonderful when he placed a hand on her thigh.

All at once she realized how drunk she was. She looked up at the ceiling and the room began to spin. Or was it the sofa? She had to grab his arm to stop herself from tumbling onto the floor; he stared at her in surprise.

"Are you okay?"

"I think…This is embarrassing, but I think I've had too much to drink."

There was kindness in his eyes. "No problem. Would you like me to walk you home?"

"I'd rather go on my own. But thanks. Thanks, Robban."

He accompanied her into the hallway, where she fumbled with her shoes and jacket, then he gave her a hug and said goodnight. She had only gone the length of the garden path leading to the road, where a sparse lilac hedge separated the grass from the tarmac on the other side, when she threw up. There wasn't a soul in sight, it was pitch-dark beyond the pools of light from the streetlamps; the smells were different out here from in the city, earthy, grass, dampness, rotting leaves. Nature. She vomited again, overwhelmed by an intense surge of shame and embarrassment. She couldn't remember when she had last drunk so much that she threw up. She looked around; the area was still deserted.

She tried to creep into her parents' house, but the place was a minefield of creaking doors and floorboards, and the glasses in the kitchen cupboard rattled as she clumsily reached for one.

"Karolina?" came her mother's voice from the bedroom.

It took her straight back to being a teenager, sneaking in late, sometimes just as drunk as she was now. Her mother had always stayed awake until she knew Karolina was safely home.

"Yes, I'm back."

"Sleep well."

At eleven o'clock the following day she had to drag herself downstairs, where her parents were already drinking their mid-morning coffee. They didn't say anything, but one look in the bathroom mirror made it clear that she couldn't hide her hangover. She fell asleep on the sofa, woke up when it was time for lunch, and forced down a few mouthfuls of the expensive smoked salmon her parents had bought in Valdemarsvik.

I can't keep doing this, she thought. My life is pathetic. Something has to change.

It was a mild fall. The late summer was over, and she was glad. It was the uneasiest time of the year, August and early September, with its satiated late summer light, the sea changing from the cobalt blue of June and July to a darker Prussian blue, the vegetation darkening, mute and harsh, turning black in the shadow of the leaves. There was a streak of cruelty about the whole thing, something almost nightmarish.

The fall was kinder, and this particular fall was unusually gentle, longing for company. The fig tree she had bought and placed on the balcony as soon as she moved in still had green leaves and looked as if it was happy there, in spite of the fact that the balcony faced onto the courtyard, where the sun found its way for only a few hours each day. It was damp out there; the air seemed to stand still. Maybe it was a bit like a greenhouse, or the Mediterranean climate, even though it was mostly in the shade. The little tree had put on a considerable amount of growth in just a few months. One branch was a lot longer than the others; it was the one closest to the railings, and had been exposed to the most sun. She should have turned the pot around occasionally. Now the tree was no longer symmetrical, it looked odd, with that long branch reaching out toward the light.

She fetched the kitchen scissors and snipped it off above a leaf nodule so that all the branches were of roughly equal length. It was a lovely branch; she liked the shape of the leaves, and she now realized that she also liked the smell of the fig tree: a white liquid was seeping from the cut surface, releasing the most wonderful aroma. As if the color green had a scent—sharp and grassy, yet at the same time sweet and milky. Maybe that was how chlorophyll smelled. It was the essence of sunshine and greenery, photosynthesis—life itself, in fact.

When she got to the university Gunilla's leaving party was going on in the lunchroom; Karolina had forgotten all about it. She lingered in the doorway for a few seconds contemplating the cross-section of staff who were determinedly mingling, clutching a plastic glass of sparkling wine and canapés from Picard. Peter Tallfalk caught sight of her and beckoned her in, but she shook her head and pulled a face to indicate that she was stressed. She wasn't stressed at all, she just didn't feel like socializing. She had come in to print out some articles about Ilya Ivanov, but as soon as she sat down at the computer, Anton stuck his head around the door. He was wearing a jacket that looked a little too big; she guessed he'd picked it up from a secondhand shop. She also guessed that he was unfamiliar with what she had come to realize was an important aspect of gentlemen's outfitting: taking one's jacket to a tailor and having it altered so that it fit perfectly.

"...and one of them is very similar to Acke's *Forest Temple,*" she heard him say as she realized she had forgotten to listen, and had simply been staring at him as he spoke, his cheekbones and chin, clearly delineated in what was still a cherubic face. There was something about his features that softened it, the curve of his lips...

"Oh, that's interesting," she said vaguely. "It's generally regarded as something pretty unique in the history of Swedish art."

"Maybe it's more of a coincidence rather than a sign of the influence of Symbolism?" he said. "I mean, Acke's other paintings are totally different. You know, those naked men by the sea."

She nodded.

"Perhaps an experiment rather than a coincidence. A whim. Like Georg von Rosen's *Sphinx*. Have you seen it?"

He shook his head.

"It's such a funny mixture of historic painting and symbolism. Executed with total realism."

"Just like sphinxes in reality," he shot back.

She laughed. He looked so sweet in his ill-fitting jacket.

"There's a brilliant essay on how you can see echoes of Mallarmé in the works of Bruno Liljefors, which makes some of his bird paintings in particular into a kind of symbolism. It's pretty bold, but very convincing, and beautifully written. I've got a copy here somewhere..."

She stood up and went over to the bookshelf where she kept her folders. Once upon a time she'd had a proper system, but it had collapsed long ago. She thought the essay was in a blue folder, and grabbed one at random.

She didn't say anything as she turned the pages. Suddenly she had the feeling that he was watching her. She looked up and saw that she was right; he was indeed gazing at her with his crooked little smile. Was she making a fool of herself in some way? What if he had no interest in reading an essay on symbolism in a painting of ducks, who the hell would be interested in that? Apart from her. What if he thought she was boring? It was a foolish notion, you don't do a PhD in a subject that doesn't appeal to you, and she was an authority on this specific topic, it was reasonable to assume that he would want to hear what she had to say. And even if he did think she was boring, why should she care?

In her dealings with Anton so far she had gotten the impression that he was typical of his generation, in that he never showed his inferiority. He never allowed her to feel that she knew more than him, but she had also noticed that beneath the cool facade he was absorbing every word she said, possibly so that he could use it himself in a different context in order to impress someone else. She had met his sort before, those who displayed a parasitic behavior that was flattering at the same time; she liked the idea that both Anton and other postgraduates and undergraduates would go out into the world and use her thoughts and phrases as if they themselves had come up with them. It was as if the process elevated her ideas to the status of universal truths.

At the moment, however, she was unsure of him. The possibility that his lack of interest was genuine made her feel stressed, and irritated, and something else. Curious? Excited? She didn't know.

She finally found the right folder and took out a black and white booklet with two wild ducks on the front.

"It's well worth reading," she said as she handed it to him.

"You can hardly see the birds," he said sulkily.

Which was true. The booklet was a copy of a copy of a copy of a copy, and the picture on the front was more or less a black blur.

"It's hanging in the Thiel Gallery."

"Just like Acke's *Forest Temple*?"

She nodded.

"It's high time I went there," Anton mumbled.

"Have you never been?"

She could hear how surprised she sounded—almost appalled, in fact. He gave a nervous laugh. At last she felt as if she was in control of the situation.

"I've only been living here for a few months," he said quietly, with a touch of embarrassment.

"You really should go one weekend," she said kindly. "It's a lovely outing."

"It would be good to go with you."

He was staring straight at her; she had to look away.

It would be weird going on a private trip with a PhD student, possibly even inappropriate. No one had ever suggested such a thing before. A visit to the Thiel Gallery was usually scheduled as part of the advanced course, but of course Anton hadn't done his degree in Stockholm.

"I'm not sure..." she began, before he interrupted her.

"Have you got anything planned for this afternoon? Any meetings?"

"No."

"So couldn't we go now? I've got a car."

His smile was so triumphant that she couldn't help smiling too.

"You've got a car? Here?"

"It's in the parking lot at Lappis. It belongs to a friend, but he lets me use it. It'll take me ten minutes to go and pick it up—fifteen max."

She looked out of the window. This might be the last fine day of the fall. She really ought to do something other than work on such a lovely day.

"Okay. If you fetch the car, we'll go to the gallery."

He wasn't a very good driver, but maybe that was because he wasn't used to the city. Karolina had to act as navigator, telling him which lane to choose and where to turn. It was nice, and he had no hang-ups about his crappy driving. They chatted and laughed; when they reached Djurgården the leaves sparkled like gold in the autumn sun, she was having fun. It was such a long time since she'd had fun.

And it was fun showing him around the gallery. It was as if the whole world contracted until there was only this moment, this place, inside the old exhibition rooms. Munch's powerful portrait of Nietzsche, the heightened, suffocating sensation in Richard Bergh's *The Knight and the Maiden*, Eugène Jansson's swirling blue twilights. They spent a long time in front of Acke's *Forest Temple*; Anton contemplated it in silence, then eventually he said appreciatively: "That's one weird painting."

He sounded so thrilled that his words went straight to her heart. And he was absolutely right, it was one weird painting. That was why she loved the whole epoch around the turn of the twentieth century, the sex, the drugs, the oppressive atmosphere, the vague sense of something unpleasant. It was all pretty weird.

She had often thought in recent years that she had a typical addictive personality, and that her drugs of choice were alcohol, sex and art. At the lowest point of her relationship with Karl

Johan, she had been cheating on him with two men at the same time. She sometimes pictured life as an electricity grid of attractions, with people ricocheting back and forth, where nothing is constant or clear. Sometimes we are fooled into thinking that it is, that others' relationships are resting on solid ground, but there is almost always a gap. Nothing is fixed, and the cracks were often there right from the start. Those glances around the room in so many contexts that say "I would cheat on my wife with you tonight, if you're interested. Do you want to? Do you also have someone you'd like to cheat on? Or someone you want to forget?"

She had said yes a few times, that was how she had met the two men, one after a lecture she had given at the Workers' Educational Society, the other at a private viewing. She hadn't really felt anything for either of them, but their appreciation had made her feel good, their bodies made her feel less lonely for a while. It was both deceptive and short-lived, like when you eat candy because you're hungry and really ought to eat proper food, but in that moment candy is better than nothing. At the same time she had filled in an online questionnaire, just for fun, which was supposed to tell you if you were in the risk zone for sexual abuse. She had gotten quite a high score and was advised to talk to someone, which of course she hadn't done, but it was still in the back of her mind.

The thing that bothered her most was the fact that she gained no real pleasure from any of her addictions these days. The first sip of wine always put her in a good mood, which lasted to the bottom of the glass, but then things went rapidly downhill if she was drinking alone. If she had company the good mood lasted longer, sometimes until she lost track of how much she'd drunk,

but the angst the following day meant that she was miserable anyway. As far as art was concerned, she had long since realized that
nothing gave her the same buzz she had experienced fifteen or
twenty years ago. It was those powerful reactions that had guided
her career choice, but there was very little of that joy, that overwhelming, dizzying sensation within the framework of her job,
among the e-mails to be answered, the tests to be marked, the
teaching and the mentoring. It wasn't even there in her research.
Occasionally she recaptured it for a fleeting moment, when she
was traveling and saw a picture she had never seen before in a
gallery in another country, but it happened very rarely.

When she witnessed Anton's undisguised delight at *Forest
Temple* and Bruno Liljefors' wild ducks, and then the heavy,
muted painting of a flight of eider ducks above an immense gray-
green wave, she was happy. She didn't know what else to call it;
she was filled with real happiness, seeing him utterly gripped by
the birds, the water, the wave, the art. At the same time she envied
him because he still had access to that feeling, because it was so
easily evoked. She would have liked to see the paintings through
his eyes. Not just the paintings. The whole world.

They were standing very close together on the staircase below
the huge canvas, she was aware of his smell, light and fresh, she
wanted to lean even closer. The listless autumn sunshine seeped
in through the windows, but was swallowed up by the dark wood,
the curtains and rugs. Dust motes danced in the air, and there
was silence all around them; the only sound she could hear was
Anton's breathing. She wanted to reach out and touch him; she
tried to suppress the urge, but it refused to go away. He had taken
off his jacket; he was wearing a white shirt with the sleeves rolled
up, his forearms were tanned and muscular, the skin on the inside

looked incredibly soft. She wanted to run her fingertips along the inside of his arm. Yes. That was all she wanted to do.

Suddenly a curator appeared at the top of the stairs. "We're closing shortly," he informed them.

They left the gallery in silence, walked slowly toward the car. She felt dizzy, almost drunk. When he offered to drive her home she refused at first, it was out of his way, he could drop her off somewhere in Östermalm, but he insisted, said he needed to practice his driving anyway. All the way to Söder he talked about various books he needed to read for his dissertation, asking her if she had them. She did have a copy of the first one, but it was in her office at the university, which annoyed him.

"Well, do you have a biography of Max Klinger?"

"I don't think so."

"Phillippe Jullian's book on Symbolism?"

"Yes, but I think that's probably at work too."

"What about the catalogue from that exhibition on German Symbolism at Waldemarsudde? You know the one I mean?"

It was obvious what he was after, even if she hardly dared believe it.

"Yes...yes, I've got that one."

"Can I borrow it?" he said immediately.

"Isn't it in the library?" she said, testing him.

"All the copies are out."

It was such a blatant lie that she had to smile. There was no chance that all the copies of a fifteen-year-old exhibition catalogue were out on loan.

"Of course you can borrow it. No problem."

When he had found a parking space by Ersta Hospital, they stood close together in the cramped, grinding elevator up to her apartment. She fumbled for her keys, found them at last and let him in. It was weird, she thought when he was in the middle of her living room, as if something she could never have imagined was actually happening. He seemed pleased, and looked around with interest.

"Nice bookshelves."

"Thanks. Can I get you something? Coffee, water? Wine?"

"Wine?"

He repeated the word with an upward inflexion, as if he wasn't sure she was really offering him a glass of wine, then he nodded.

Needless to say, she shouldn't be offering a PhD student wine. If they did happen to have a drink together for some reason, it should be in a bar, or possibly in her apartment with a group of other people, colleagues or fellow students perhaps. And if a PhD student wanted to borrow a book, she should take it to the university, hand it over in a formal environment in the department.

She went into the kitchen and got out two glasses. She took a bottle of white wine out of the refrigerator and opened a tin of black olives. Back in the living room Anton was leafing through a book on the aesthetic movement in England. She sat down beside him on the sofa and poured the wine. He immediately took a huge gulp, and it struck her that he might be nervous.

"Lovely apartment," he said.

"Thanks. I haven't lived here for very long, but I like it. I like the whole building."

"Yes, it's great."

"The only problem is that they haven't made a very good job of renovating the stairwell."

Good God, what was she saying? Anton took another swig of his wine.

"Really? I didn't notice."

"They spray-painted the walls. I don't like spray-painted walls. It looks like a bicycle storage shed."

"Or like quails' eggs."

Quails' eggs. What a strange idea.

The sun shining in through the window lit up his hair like a halo. There was something of the Renaissance about his appearance, especially his beautifully chiseled lips. Like one of the young men in the choir of angels in Botticelli's painting in the Gemäldegalerie in Berlin. Something pure, something inaccessible, which should also be inaccessible to her; the university took a serious line when it came to sexual liaisons. If he told anyone in the department about their day together, claiming that it had been her idea, that she had persuaded him to come back to her place, that would be the end of her career.

She ought to ask him to leave. This was a mistake.

As she turned to tell him exactly that, he leaned over and kissed her. A tentative kiss, like a question brushing against her lips. God, he looked so young. She pushed her face closer to his in answer to his question, allowed him to take the initiative and kiss her again.

He started it, she thought childishly.

His mouth tasted slightly acidic, like olives, his hands moved eagerly over her body when he plucked up the courage to touch her. She had expected something else, a sense of obligation, the idea that he was doing this because he felt he had to—or out of pity, in the worst-case scenario. She had at least expected him to be blasé, so used to women's bodies that he was bored by now; she imagined that they were offered to him everywhere. All he had to do was choose from the beautiful twenty-year-olds in the student bar or at a party as he stood in the kitchen holding court, young and good-looking and so talented, he must be regarded as a catch by women of all ages. For someone like Anton Strömberg, the female sex must be laid out before him like a continent to be explored. He could simply help himself, depending on how he felt on any given day, men too perhaps, also of all ages, he could experience whatever he wanted with just about anybody. The world must seem like an enormous promise to him, as if it had been put together with him in mind, and now it was just waiting for him.

And yet he had chosen her.

When she dared to slip her hands beneath his shirt, his body felt so different that it took her breath away. It was smooth and slender, but somehow compact and powerful at the same time. She ran her hand over his stomach; he didn't have a six-pack, but it was still firm, held together by the biology that hadn't yet added a few extra pounds, unaffected by the gravity that within a precisely measured period of time would make his body begin to sag. His eyes gleamed, almost cat-like in the last rays of the evening sun; the smell of him was unmistakable at such close quarters. Youth, she thought. This is what youth smells like.

He had gone when she woke up. She didn't want to get out of bed, where the pillow beside her still bore traces of his smell. Her whole body felt sated and indolent, well-rested yet sleepy, like a cat dozing in the sun.

In spite of the undeniable inappropriateness of the whole thing, it had been a good evening, maybe even wonderful. They had made love on the sofa, quickly and passionately, then he had grabbed the throw from the armrest and pulled it over them. They had lain there talking and finishing off the wine, she had fetched another bottle and they had drunk that too as he wandered along her bookshelves, wide-eyed, pulling out a book, sitting on the sofa and flicking through it, commenting on the pictures, getting up to choose another one, leafing through that, as carefree as a child. He had gone through her playlists on the computer and chosen one, told her how good it was, some of the tracks were among his favorites. They had gotten just drunk enough, flirting happily, and she had felt turned on by the kind of positive affirmation she hadn't received since she was his age, the fact that someone liked the books she had, told her she had good taste in music—it was banal, but she still liked it, at least in this pleasant state of intoxication. They had made love again, in the bedroom this time, slowly and tenderly, and had stayed in bed. He had told her about his childhood, his single mom, and she had loved every word. "I still don't think she really understands what I do," he had said. "But she's very proud of the fact that I'm at university. She didn't even go to high school." The conversation had drifted into his dissertation and his stay in Berlin, he had talked at length about his meetings with Lotte Baumann, which made Karolina feel very affectionate toward him. He spoke about the old lady with such respect and appreciation. Then they had fallen asleep, their bodies close.

She would have liked to know what mood he had been in as he silently moved around her apartment gathering up his things, closing the door behind him without waking her. He hadn't left a note, or any trace of himself. He hadn't texted her.

Had he looked down at her as she slept? What had he thought? She was afraid he might have regretted his actions, afraid that the merciless morning light had made him realize she was old and unattractive, made him think, "Oh my God, what have I done?" before he hurried away, full of disgust and self-loathing.

However, nothing could affect the joy she felt because he had chosen her, in spite of everything. He had taken the initiative to come home with her, and to kiss her. She couldn't stop smiling at the knowledge that someone like Anton clearly found her attractive.

He wasn't in the department the following day, but that wasn't unusual; most days he didn't come in. She went past his room; the door was open and there was still next to nothing on his desk, apart from a couple of untidy piles of papers and an unwashed coffee cup.

After a quick glance over her shoulder, she stepped inside.

Yes, there it was. The smell.

In the lunchroom she bumped into Lennart Olsson. She had even more of a problem with him since that look he had given her in his apartment. What annoyed her most was the fact that he had looked at her in a way that made it clear he thought he had a chance with her. He had far too much self-confidence.

"Anton Strömberg's research is really exciting," she said to him, as if in passing. "His material is much more interesting than I could have imagined."

Lennart was immediately all ears.

"Oh? What's he come up with?"

Karolina reached for a cup, then pressed the button for black coffee.

"He seems to have found evidence suggesting that it was actually Ebba Ellis who gave Franz von Stuck the idea for the motif of the women with snakes—you know the ones I mean? And that they had a fascinating exchange, on both an artistic and an intellectual level. It looks as if there's a link between Sweden and German Symbolism that has never been researched."

Lennart was staring at her as if he couldn't believe his ears. She could understand that. And she could imagine the thoughts that were whirling around inside his head, the envy, the resentment from someone who always thinks he deserves the best. She smiled as she picked up her cup of coffee.

"It's so much fun to be involved in this," she said. "It's the kind of thing that comes along only once in a lifetime."

She walked away, filled with an intoxicating rush of triumph. It made her walk tall; she felt invincible. It lasted all the way into the room where she was due to give the first lecture of the semester, and while she greeted the students who had already arrived. Most of them looked young, and they probably were; this was part of the foundation course, which meant that some of them might have graduated from high school less than a year ago. They were a quiet group; they didn't appear to know one another, and didn't really chat as she set up her computer and made sure the slideshow was working. She clicked through on the screen; it was very good. She knew it always went down well, and that was exactly what she wanted; she was determined that no one should leave the first lecture wondering if they'd chosen the wrong course.

By one o'clock the room was almost full. No more than twenty students, most looking expectant, the odd one with an air of nonchalance, but she could tell this was a good group. Nobody was too nervous when she did a brief sweep of the room, asking each person to introduce themselves, and when she asked a few questions about previous courses, several were quick to volunteer answers. She went over some practical details about the syllabus and reading material, answered a query about exams, then she dimmed the lights, brought up the slideshow and explained that she was intending to give an introduction to the various themes that would be covered during the course.

She began with the background to the epoch on which they would be focusing, and went in hard with Courbet's *The Origin of the World*, a close-up view of the genitals and abdomen of a naked woman, lying on a bed with her legs spread. She thought it would capture the attention of her audience. Then she moved on to a series of paintings by the pre-Raphaelites—Millais' *Ophelia* and Dante Gabriel Rossetti's red-haired women—and some academic painters, Bouguereau, Rochegrosse, Cabanel. She paused at Cabanel's Venus, lying on her back on a foaming green wave, surrounded by cherubs.

"We'll be returning to this painting," she said as everyone made a note, one or two looking worried because they hadn't been listening carefully and had missed the artist's name.

Then she clicked through various examples of motifs: woman as a good mother, the angel within the home. Woman as nature. Woman with different kinds of animals. Woman *as* different kinds of animals. Woman as sphinx and vampire. Woman as siren and femme fatale. The fallen woman. The lesbian woman. The madwoman. The sick and sleeping woman. The drowned and dead woman. Woman as death.

It really was a good introduction; she was very pleased with it. The gathering darkness, the increasingly twisted images. Her cheeks were flushed as she approached the final section.

"I want you to remember," she said, "that we can't demand the political correctness of today from pictures that are a hundred and twenty, a hundred and thirty years old. We're not here to decide that the artists back then had an unacceptable view of women, and that these pictures are appalling. We are here to understand why they look as they do."

She quickly ran through a series of photographs and drawings illustrating the cultural and social phenomena that would form the basis for the art they would be studying: industrialization, urbanization, prostitution and the widespread proliferation of syphilis in the cities, secularization, Darwin's theories, the women's movement, Freud.

The final picture was the French symbolist Gustav-Adolf Mossa's monumental *Elle*, which portrayed a gigantic naked woman with large breasts, perched on top of a pile of tiny people. If you looked closely, you could see that they were bloody male corpses. Her eyes were cold, and there was a little devil curled up between her thighs.

Karolina could see a spectrum of emotions on her students' faces when she switched on the light: some were torn, their initial reaction was no doubt to dismiss the paintings as sexist, yet at the same time they were fascinated, not unreceptive to the alternative view she had put to them: When in the history of art had women ever been depicted as stronger than during this epoch? When had men ever perceived them as being so terrifying, so powerful, capable of both giving and taking life, the rulers of the home, yet at the same time on their way toward power within society through the progress of the women's movement? The misogyny that was often cited as an explanation for the art of that particular epoch was in fact the fear of women, just as the last picture had illustrated. Admittedly it wasn't ideal, but personally Karolina would much rather be feared than hated. In a seminar later in the

140

semester she would raise the question of whether there were similar tendencies in contemporary art, bearing in mind that women now formed the majority at colleges and universities, while poorly educated men in small communities were today's losers. And was there a link to the misogyny that flourished on the Internet, a constant reference point in the debate on society? Could this also be seen as an expression of the fear of women, in a parallel to the last century? She was looking forward to the discussions.

She was lost in thought as she headed back to the lunchroom for coffee.

"I need to call in at the bakery as well," she heard a woman at one of the tables say.

"Absolutely. We should have ordered a box of buns to go with our afternoon coffee. We must do that next year."

"Have you had a bun, Karolina?"

She gave a start when she heard her name; she looked over at the two women who were drinking coffee at a table by the window.

"Sorry?"

"It's cinnamon bun day!" said Lisbet Hedlund, a PhD in children's literature and something of an authority on the subject. Jungian, as all those who specialized in children's books seemed to be, and constantly on her way to a panel meeting for some impending prize or bursary award, to a conference in Poland or the book fair in Bologna. There was nothing wrong with Lisbet, she was a sweetheart, but sometimes she seemed to have no connection whatsoever with reality.

"Oh really? I . . . I forgot."

"Don't you think we should order a box of cinnamon buns next year?" said Anna-Lena Lindén, whose field was the history of ideas. She sounded as if it really mattered.

"Yes. Definitely. Good idea."

Who the hell cares whether or not it's cinnamon bun day, Karolina thought as she walked back to her office. Then she burst into tears, which came as something of a shock; she had to hurry into her room and close the door. She sat at her desk sobbing and shaking, her tears splashing onto a book about Fra Angelico.

She hated cinnamon bun day, because it hurt too much to enjoy it. You can only enjoy days like that in the company of others. What if she bought a bun, took it home, poured herself a cup of coffee and thought, "I'm celebrating cinnamon bun day, isn't this lovely?"

How sad would that be? She cried even harder.

Self-pity, she tried to tell herself. It's nothing more than self-pity. But she would have loved to have someone to eat a bun with, someone to laugh with over how silly the idea of such a day was, but she would still buy two buns to take home in a slightly ironic way, because of course nobody really cares about something like cinnamon bun day, but they do taste good.

The joy she had felt earlier in the day, the strong sense of total affirmation after the night with Anton, had disappeared completely. That wasn't what she wanted, deep down. She wanted someone who wanted her. Someone who liked her enough to think about a future together.

In a feeble attempt to exercise, she had started taking a walk in the evenings. She hated the gym and she didn't enjoy running; anything that required a change of clothing and a shower was too much effort. Her walks demanded no more than the humiliation that went with wearing sneakers in the city, but it didn't seem to bother anyone in Södermalm, so she carried on along Folkungagatan down to the London Viaduct, took a right down the cycle track and past the warehouse at Danvikstull, then along the quayside toward Skanstull. Sometimes she went farther, on to Tantolunden and Hornstull before turning for home in the twilight. She had to set off earlier each evening, and she knew she would soon have to stop. Once winter came it would be difficult to fit in a walk; she wouldn't want to follow that same route in the dark.

"It is the middle of the day in Goethe's poetry," she had read in an essay recently, a comparison between the classical and Romantic artistic temperament, a clear image that had stuck in her mind. It is twilight in Nietzsche's work, twilight in Baudelaire, twilight in the work of everyone with whom she felt an affinity. But in Goethe's poetry it was the middle of the day. She pictured it in her mind's eye: the light, the beauty. Fresh breezes, fresh ideas. A marble white temple perched high on a rock, supported by rows of strong columns, shimmering, clean and pure.

She paused in front of the colossal buildings in Tanto, five gigantic, semicircular apartment blocks from the late modernist era. She had always found them brutal, bordering on grotesque, insensitively located right next to picturesque community gardens. Suddenly she saw the classicism in them, a concrete Colosseum, gladiatorial contests and roaring lions, the naval battles in the flooded arena, the metallic smell of blood in the air. They would make glorious ruins: the crumbling curves covered in ivy and wild vines, a few rabbits hopping around, oblivious to the decay. She had always imagined that she would stand on the highest point in Tanto when the apocalypse came, a second after she had thought, "That's funny, there are two suns in the sky" and the blast wave came surging in over Södermalm, shattering the windows in the modernist dream around her, people didn't even have time to scream.

Utopias scared her, the kind embodied within the challenging and uncompromising benevolence represented by the buildings before her, but maybe that was a bad reaction, completely wrong for someone like her, with her temperament and psychological disposition, someone who was all too ready to become submerged in her own feelings as if they were a stinking bog. We should all believe in something, something bigger than ourselves. What do we believe in in the absence of God, in the absence of ideologies and communities?

She thought about Gavriila and the ape. It wasn't that hard to understand after all.

Beneath the old Årsta Bridge she turned for home; a small group of teenage punks were drinking beer on the grass in a last desperate attempt to deny that it was fall now. On the way back she gazed across the water at the Hammarbybacken ski resort, almost blue in the hazy air; it reminded her of a Renaissance painting. The slopes had been made using material excavated during the construction of the Ericsson Globe and the Hammarby marina. It was known as a ruderal or brownfield site, land which was the result of human activity, rubbish dumps and industrial areas, a biotope created by man that has been reclaimed by nature's inexorable cycle and produced its own bizarre flora. It seemed that virtually anything could grow among the grass and undergrowth and goose grass, plants that had arrived in the form of garbage but had flourished in the soil. There were overgrown sunflowers and tomatoes, but more exotic species such as date palms and avocados could shoot up in this ecological free zone. Ugly, but life-affirming.

In that way Hammarbybacken was a million miles from the stunningly beautiful mountains of Renaissance art, but they too were sometimes man-made, in a different way. Bruegel's mountaintops did not exist in the Dutch landscape in which he placed them in his work. He had seen them as a young man in Italy, and sneaked a little bit of Palermo, Naples and Rome into the background of those snowy Dutch views.

She pictured Petrarch on his way up Hammarbybacken instead of Mont Ventoux, ascending the Renaissance itself, reaching the top as a modern man. She had once visited the Amalfi coast with Karl Johan. They had signed up for a coach trip to Mount Vesuvius, because he refused to drive in southern Europe, and they had walked the last stretch in the thin, misty, increasingly chilly air. The slopes had been covered in a proliferation of mimosa in full bloom, like a bright yellow foam on waves rolling in toward an island, and all the way to the top they had been surrounded by the smell of sulfur and mimosa, which she would remember forever. And when they stood at the summit, broken off like a jagged tooth with all the miasma of the innards surging up from far below, she had looked down at the sparkling waters of the Bay of Naples and felt something that might actually have been happiness.

It is full daylight in Goethe's poetry. And in Petrarch's it is dawn. She thought of the early Renaissance as the morning of modern man, as the spring of the culture she loved. She wanted to live there, in the sun, in the light. The halcyon days. The way she had felt when she lay beside Anders.

Why hadn't she fought for him? Why had she let him go, someone who made her feel happy and harmonious; why had she gone home to a relationship that was utterly meaningless? How could two adults throw away something that was so genuine and so rare?

The thought became even more unbearably real when she got back to her stuffy apartment, the faint odor of bodies still lingering in the air. The wineglasses she and Anton had used still stood on the coffee table, the olives had dried out and cracked, like a Baroque still life on transience. The whole thing felt sordid.

How she longed for something pure.

She picked up her cell phone.

He might not even have the same number anymore. And even if he had, he might not answer. If the worst came to the worst, he would be dismissive. Angry, perhaps. Angry because she had destroyed his life, although that would be an unfair accusation; he had been as committed to their affair as she had, equally absorbed by it, equally keen to meet, equally unwilling to part each time he had to leave. But he could easily have seen things in a different light afterward; his wife might have made him see Karolina as a grotesque mistake. Had he spent the last few years regretting the whole thing, wishing they'd never met, wishing they'd never gone down that side street after the dinner at the National Museum and discovered that it was impossible to stop kissing each other? Maybe he was happy with his Mikaela; Karolina had seen a photograph of her when he was scrolling through the pictures on his phone to show her his children. To be honest, she had no interest in seeing his children; she actually found the idea unpleasant. Two small people who looked like him, but not just him—the woman with whom he had chosen to build a family. Alice and Elliot, catching crabs on a jetty in Bohuslän. Gappy, happy smiles, life jackets, plastic buckets, and Mikaela, a pretty woman a few years younger than Karolina, tanned and beaming into the camera in a brightly colored summer dress, her hair in a thick braid. She looked like a wife. If someone had asked Karolina to describe a wife, she would have described her exactly like Mikaela: she looked pretty and ordinary, yet there was a firmness, a determination about her that Karolina had realized many men found attractive—or at least they got used to it. As Anders had done. Besides which, he and Mikaela had met when they were very young and had grown together; he was perfectly happy in his everyday life with her. It wasn't particularly good, but it wasn't particularly bad either. Not until Karolina destroyed it.

She weighed the phone in her hand.

"Hi?" she wrote, then quickly pressed "send" before she had time to change her mind.

The silence in the apartment became even more dense; she could almost hear it, as if a creature was lurking somewhere, absorbing every sound. She turned up the volume of her phone as loud as it would go, then she switched on the radio in the kitchen, keeping it low. There was a discussion program on P1, it spread through the apartment like an antidote to the silence. She washed the wineglasses, threw away the shriveled olives and washed the bowl. The branch from the fig tree, which she had placed in a vase on the living room table, had withered and died. She broke it up and put it in the trash.

At long last a text message came through. The mere sight of the name Anders on the display made her feel a little sick.

"Hi ☺" it said.

He had never used smileys before, but she understood why he had sent one now, and it made her happy—more than happy, in fact. In a second all her anxiety was gone, she was slightly dizzy, her cheeks were burning, she wanted to throw her arms around him, kiss him, lose herself in his embrace, never let him go again.

Her phone pinged again. "How are you?" he wondered. How was she? She had to think about that for a moment.

"I miss you," she replied.

She had opened the sluice gates of her emotions, acknowledged something that had been lying dormant within her for over a year. She might scare him, but at least she would have tried. He might think it was too much, that she should have sent a polite, superficial response, but nothing in their relationship had been polite or superficial. It had been honest, as honest as a relationship based on lies can be, but they had never lied to one another. She actually remembered thinking that during one of their encounters in a hotel room: she couldn't ever imagine lying to him, she who cheerfully lied to everyone; she regarded it as one of her talents.

He came back right away.

"I miss you too."

She lay down on the sofa, took a deep breath. She felt weirdly light and heavy at the same time; was it anticipation? Arousal? Longing?

She didn't know what to write next, she didn't want to seem pushy or desperate. Although of course she was desperate. What a sad realization. Nobody wants a desperate woman. She had read a piece in one of the gossip mags about a beautiful and successful Hollywood actress who "couldn't hold on to a man," as the article had put it. She's nearly forty and she's desperate, the writer had said, men can smell it and they run a mile. It was a horrible way of putting it, which was why it had stuck in Karolina's mind. Maybe it was true. Maybe loneliness surrounded her too like a bad smell, making everyone who perceived it recoil.

She put down the phone and reached for a pile of papers on the coffee table: articles about Ilya Ivanov and his experiments with apes. Soon she had read everything the Internet had to offer on the project, including those pages maintaining that the whole thing had been an attempt to produce an ape-man to use in war, an ultra-aggressive soldier with low intelligence and animalistic instincts. Stalin had allegedly demanded "a living war machine": tough, oblivious to pain, indifferent to any circumstances, including psychological pressure. Such an army would be invincible.

The more serious essays on the subject denied that there had been any such purpose behind the experiment, or simply didn't mention it. There was nothing more about the woman, G. Gavriila.

Karolina pictured her in a room that had been prepared for her at the research facility in Georgia. She actually came from Leningrad, that was the only piece of information Karolina had managed to find out about her. Had she lived there all her life, and moved because of the experiment? There was nothing to cling to in her past; her life was in ruins because of things that had gone wrong. Failure, unhappiness. She might have considered killing herself, or entering a convent. Instead she chose to put herself in the hands of science—an equally significant sacrifice, but simultaneously an investment for the whole of humanity.

She must have been afraid and she must have hesitated, but it had seemed like a calling greater than herself, something she simply had to do, in spite of the many risks that had been spelled out to her. No one knew how her body would react to the alien element that would grow in her womb. And what would happen when she gave birth? Her life would be in danger with every step she took, she knew that. But she had trusted Dr. Ivanov. He had been kind to her, and he was grateful that she had volunteered. It had felt like the two of them against the world; they were a team, and they understood each other.

Ivanov set up a meticulous system in order to monitor her fertility: tables, diaries, charts. His assistant made a note of her temperature several times a day. She had always had regular periods; perhaps that was one reason why she had been selected. She was biologically reliable. When nothing else was working, her body still did what it was supposed to do.

Her room had probably been pretty basic, as if she really were in a convent cell. She might have brought a few personal items in addition to her clothes and toiletries. Some books. The odd piece of jewelry. A photograph of someone she wanted to remember, in spite of everything?

How did she spend her days? Walking by the sea, reading? What did she read? No doubt she had been served nutritious food to make her strong: meat, fresh fish, fruit and vegetables. Had she exchanged letters with anyone while she was there? Did anyone from her old life know what she was doing? Or had she kept it entirely to herself? If so, that must have been the epitome of loneliness.

And what had she thought about? At night, before she went to sleep. When she lay in her bed, her mind whirling. Had she been convinced, even in those moments? Or had she begun to have doubts? Tried to push her worries aside, tried not to cry. Gritted her teeth, told herself this was how it had to be. Because there was nothing else.

A desperate woman.

The phone on the table pinged. Karolina gave a start, grabbed it. A message from Anders: "How about meeting up sometime?"

There was no need for them to meet in a hotel; that alone was staggering. She rushed frantically around the apartment before he arrived, trying to see it through his eyes. She straightened up the books on the shelves, some were pushed in farther than others, they looked messy. She picked the yellow leaves off the potted plants on the windowsills. She opened the balcony door to let the fresh air sweep in; she didn't want the place to smell stuffy. She contemplated the paintings on the walls, the still-life arrangements of ornaments and small sculptures she had set out on a cupboard and a chest of drawers, did they look stupid? As if she had made too much of an effort to make the place look like something from an interiors magazine? The little owl from a museum store—too kitsch?

She had thought about nothing but Anders since they had arranged to meet. Everything else in her life, including the evening with Anton, seemed irrelevant by comparison. He still hadn't been in touch; at first she had wondered what he was doing, what he thought of her, jealously brooded on whether he was spending his nights with someone else. Then she began to believe that the silence on his part was a positive sign; hopefully he too realized that what had happened was a mistake, however good it might have been. A mistake they had no need to regret, but there was certainly no need to repeat it either. They could simply put it behind them and move on. With a bit of luck he was busy with his dissertation, spending his days working through the collection of letters and digging out more interesting details about Ebba Ellis.

When the doorbell rang she was surprised at the sound; no one had rung the bell before. Anders looked nervous, which she found quite sweet. Maybe he also looked a little more worn, as if a gray shadow had swept across his face and settled in its corners and angles. Maybe he was thinking the same about her.

They hugged, she would have liked it to go on for longer, but he started taking off his shoes and jacket. He followed her into the living room and gazed around.

"This is lovely."

"Thanks."

"So how does it feel? Living by yourself?"

"I don't know. Lonely, if I'm honest, but it's still better than living with someone when everything feels wrong."

He nodded. "I get that."

He sat down on the sofa, and she joined him.

"Mikaela and I have split up," he went on. "We've told people it's a trial separation, but I think we both know that's not true. We each spend alternate weeks in the house with the kids, and we've rented an apartment nearby to use the rest of the time."

"Okay...so how does that feel?"

"Fucking horrendous, to tell the truth."

His expression was tortured, and she felt a sharp stab of jealousy. When he had talked about his family situation in the past he had sounded indifferent, and had often said how much more alive he felt with Karolina, how the time they spent together made him realize that this was how life ought to be. She tried to tell herself that she was being self-obsessed: of course it was hard to break up a marriage when you took that final step, above all when there were children in the picture. She had no kids, she couldn't possibly know what that was like—which in turn made her feel incredibly unimportant, and therefore annoyed. She already knew that she could never be more important than the children to someone who was a parent, so why couldn't he tell her he'd missed her, say something that would make her feel less like a person who had destroyed his life and more like a woman he actually cared about?

It took quite a lot of wine before he came out with anything along those lines, by which time she had tearfully begun to think that of course she understood how difficult it was for him, this wasn't the time to put any pressure on him, why would she do that? He was with her now, wasn't that enough? Yes, it was, she suddenly decided. She was even more certain when he put his arm around her. God, how she had missed being close to him, she felt it in her whole body, as soon as she rested her head on his chest and filled her nostrils with the smell of him, she knew she was completely safe. It was such a long time since she had felt that way. And how she had missed the way she felt when he kissed her, and they fell back on the sofa together: total security, and at the same time she was unbelievably turned on. It was magical. It was still just as magical as it had always been.

Being with him eased her mind, stilled the thoughts that were constantly dashing back and forth, bumping into one another, making her stressed, irritated, unhappy; suddenly they were calm. And his voice, with its faint Norrland accent, was like a cool cloth on her forehead. She just wanted to stay with him, become a part of him. She would give up everything if only she could go on feeling this way, she wanted to sleep with him every single night. Her dreams would be completely different then.

"I've been having a terrible dream lately," she said when they were lying in her bed. "The whole of Söder is destroyed. A ferry crashes into Katarinaberget, making the ground shake, then everything collapses, my apartment, the entire block...every single building."

He looked at her with a worried frown, then smiled.

"That's never going to happen," he said. "It's impossible. And even if it did happen, it could be fixed."

"What do you mean, fixed?"

"Buildings can always be renovated. Look at Germany— they've restored so much that was bombed during the Second World War. And then they call someone like me, and I come along and sort it all out until it looks like new...or old."

"Have you done that kind of stuff?"

"I did quite a lot of work in Germany before the children were born. They have a different attitude to restoration over there compared with Sweden. We seem to think it's ugly to try to re-create the past—kind of kitsch. We want to make it clear that what's new is new, so we prefer to rebuild or extend an old building in a completely different style. I guess the idea is that there's an honesty about it, a determination to show that the old is old and the new is new, that there's no pretense...typically Swedish. In Germany they have no problem with letting the new look old, and of course they've had significantly more old buildings in need of restoration. When I worked in Dresden—"

"You worked in Dresden?"

"Yes."

"Why have you never told me this?"

He laughed. "Because you never asked. I sometimes used to wonder whether you were actually interested in me at all; I thought maybe you were only after my body."

His tone was humorous, but the words made her feel embarrassed, because in a way he was right, and sad, because he hadn't understood that what she needed most from him was the intimacy. Hadn't he realized? Wasn't it as obvious and self-evident to him?

"Have you seen the glass factory in Dresden?" she said. "Volkswagen's showpiece?"

"How come you know about that?"

"I'm not sure... I read about it and it appealed to me."

"We ought to go to Dresden together one day," he said.

She smiled. "That would be lovely."

She could hear exactly how her response sounded: pleased but resigned, like a person who was used to planning things that will never happen. She had planned so many trips lying in bed next to so many men, and none of them—apart from holidays with Karl Johan, but then again they hadn't been planned in bed—had ever happened.

He looked at her.

"I don't have much work next week, and Mikaela will be with the kids. Maybe we should go to Dresden? If you can manage it?"

"I don't think I have anything planned that can't wait."

"I'll show you what I've done around Neumarkt. And we can take a look at the glass factory."

"Are you serious?"

"Of course I'm serious."

. . .

As she was packing she thought that for the first time she understood what people who enjoyed traveling actually liked, or even loved: the anticipation. Thinking of the future and imagining something fantastic.

In the past the only thing she had been able to imagine in connection with traveling was her own death. She still found the idea of flying unpleasant, but for different reasons. Right now even death wasn't so frightening. If she was going to die, she would die together with Anders. When the plane exploded or crashed into the sea or the side of a mountain, he would be holding her hand in his.

Such a tragedy, people would say when they heard about the accident, but in fact it wasn't a tragedy at all. That was exactly how she would want to go: the plane drawing a line across the sky, on its way into the future at speed, it is morning, they are flying south, it is bright and beautiful up above the clouds, a heavenly brightness like in a Baroque painting. Anders's hand is in hers, she is safe, contented. She thinks of the days ahead, happy days. They will make love in the hotel room before they do anything else, and this time it will be for real—not a parenthesis in a life that was actually completely different, but real life, the official version. When they finally tear themselves away from each other's body they will go out for something to eat, they will talk and laugh, the other diners will look at them and think that's the couple they'd like to be tonight, so radiantly happy.

And when her parents are informed of her death, at least they will be able to think that she was normal, going off on vacation with a man she loved, like an ordinary person with an ordinary life.

Ordinary people are so spoiled with their ordinary lives that they don't even reflect on the fact that they have them. Then they go on vacation and become the victims of a natural disaster, a terrorist attack, a terrible accident, they are obliterated, perhaps their bodies are never recovered, their friends and relatives can't believe it's true. When they are interviewed by one of the tabloid papers, which is running the story with big black headlines, they say it is an incomprehensible tragedy, but for those who die it is not an incomprehensible tragedy, because they die together. What is an incomprehensible tragedy is dying alone. She could walk out in the street, be hit by a car on Folkungagatan, be badly injured. She might hover between life and death for a while before she passed away, alone with her own brain, and one single thought: this was all that her life amounted to. With that thought she would die. Alone, with no expectations of the future.

She chose her clothes carefully, picturing each garment in the scenes she imagined the trip would involve: the days touring the city, gazing at the buildings and visiting museums and galleries, the evenings in restaurants and bars. She wanted to look as good as possible all the time, without being too dressed up; she tried on various outfits in front of the mirror in the hallway, finding clever combinations in order to save space in her suitcase. She even enjoyed fiddling about with her toiletries: she poured toner into a little plastic bottle, pumped night cream into a tiny jar, made sure everything was properly sealed, checked that it all fit into the plastic bags prescribed by the safety regulations.

It was early evening when his text message arrived; she knew it wasn't going to be good news. It was a time when he had never sent messages in the past, a time for picking up the kids and sorting out dinner, a time zone of a few hours to which she had never had access before.

Her suspicions proved well-founded.

"Mikaela wants to try again," it said. "She wants me to come and stay this week. The kids are struggling. I'm really sorry."

She wasn't even surprised. And later in the evening she thought that was the saddest part of all, the fact that she wasn't surprised. That this was the kind of person she had become, hard, atrophied inside. Next time there was a reason to be happy about something, she would try not to be. Out of a sense of self-preservation.

She tried to get mad instead, to hate him, but she couldn't do it. It might be possible in a while, she might be able to despise him eventually. Use everything he had given her in confidence against him in her head, tell herself that he was a pig, that he was disgusting. A weak, cowardly, fat guy with disagreeable political values, a guy whose hands she never wanted to feel on her body again, because the very thought of him touching her was repulsive.

But it didn't feel that way right now.

She had so wanted to go away with him, wanted this to be the beginning of something new and beautiful.

On one occasion some ten years ago, after a conference in Paris, she had stood by the luggage carousel at Arlanda waiting for her suitcase. There were plenty of people crowding around, but they quickly disappeared as the first batch arrived and they reclaimed their bags. Karolina's case wasn't in the second batch either. She had gotten frustrated, thinking this was just like another occasion when she had to wait for an eternity; it had been late at night, the airport shuttle buses had stopped running and there had been no cabs around when she finally emerged from the terminal as one of the very last passengers.

After a while there were just a few people still waiting, glancing at one another and at the aperture through which the bags would appear, all grateful that they weren't alone. As long as there were a few of them, it meant that it couldn't be just their luggage that had somehow gone missing, and if all their bags had gone missing, then at least they'd be in the same boat, and they could sort it out together.

At long last the carousel began to move, and a final batch emerged. Karolina saw the relief in the eyes of a young girl whose case was the first to appear; she ran over and dragged it onto the floor. The same thing happened for her fellow travelers, one by one they cheerfully left the silent community that had formed around the carousel. They were no longer a group; now it was up to everyone to fend for themselves. The penultimate passenger was a woman in her sixties, who beamed when her cheap red nylon suitcase arrived. She glanced at Karolina, looking a little guilty, before hurrying toward the exit, pulling the case behind her.

No more bags emerged.

And standing there beside the carousel as it continued to hum along even though it was empty, it occurred to Karolina that it was life she was waiting for. Life that came to everyone except her.

She had grown ugly, the mirror made that very clear. Only a year ago she had looked different, younger, prettier, above all fresher and more alert. Now her eyes were dead, like the eyes of someone who has stared down into the abyss and realized that it was staring right back. Not even expensive primer could do anything about that.

She hadn't bothered coloring her hair for a long time; the center parting revealed mousy roots and a few strands of gray, and when she lifted the sides she could see tens, maybe hundreds of gray hairs at her temples. She would need a lot of makeup and maybe some statement jewelry to draw attention from what she actually looked like. She sipped a glass of wine while she got ready, dabbing concealer under her eyes, applying blush in a fresh pink shade. She chose the dangly earrings; men loved dangly earrings, it was like hanging up a mobile for a baby.

Hans Jerup had managed to make the arts section's party for freelance contributors feel unfashionably glamorous by finding the budget to hire a venue, and securing sponsorship for food and drink. Writers mingled among the huge sculptures in the foyer of the Royal Academy of Fine Arts, lining up for the buffet, flocking around the small bar where a specialist supplier was offering a really good white wine. The food came from a recently opened restaurant nearby, and it was excellent. Karolina piled her plate high with tiny Asian hamburgers, packed with carrots and coriander, crispy spring rolls and a colorful salad of fennel, pomegranate and blood oranges; some poor soul had clearly been instructed to remove every scrap of the white pith. It was delicious; when had she last eaten any fruit? She couldn't remember.

She said hello in passing to the entertainment editor Hugo Zetterberg, who was the same age as her but looked ten years younger and had played in a reasonably successful band around the millennium. He was good-looking but slippery, an expert at producing articles filled with totally noncommittal views. A poser, who had cracked the code and learned how to pose as someone who has an opinion. Karolina had never been able to work out what he actually thought of her; he had always treated her with a certain wariness. Maybe he realized that she could see through him, that she thought his "A Contemporary View" pieces every Friday were utter drivel and unworthy of a man of his age.

Laura Laine, a PhD in the history of ideas and "below the line" editor, was standing at the bar chatting to Josefin Persson, who had become literature editor a year or so ago. Josefin had very little experience apart from the odd internship at a couple of arts journals, but when Karolina saw her—blonde, about thirty years old—she understood that Hans Jerup had probably seen other qualities in her that weren't on her résumé. She exchanged a few words with the two women, who were both very pleasant.

Jerup spotted her; he smiled and gave her a big hug.

"Karolina, I'm so pleased you could come." He stepped back and gazed at her, then put his mouth close to her ear. "You look fantastic," he whispered.

Was he crazy? Then again, the lighting was subdued, soft and flattering, so maybe that was why. Or maybe he was lying.

"So do you," she responded quietly.

He really did; he was well-dressed as always, a beaming host who enjoyed having guests, tapping the side of his glass and giving a little speech about how well things were going for the arts pages, how impressed the bosses were, not only over the click and share rates, but because there was some positive news as far as the hard copy was concerned, for once. Weekend subscriptions had increased significantly over the last six months, and a major reason appeared to be the substantial arts supplement that accompanied the paper on Saturdays. He emphasized the fact that each person in the room should take credit for this success, and he hoped they would all continue in the same spirit, maybe it would even be possible to pay contributors a little more—someone in the audience, possibly the architectural correspondent Peter Sundman, yelled a weary "About time!", everyone laughed—"and I want you to know how happy and proud I am to be working with the best writers in the country," Jerup said warmly. "Enjoy the food and drink, and have a good time!"

"Cheers!" shouted Hugo Zetterberg, and they all clinked glasses, Karolina with Josefin Persson and two female literary critics who happened to be nearby, before they went back to discussing the debate on sexism in the world of culture which had been running in various newspapers throughout the fall. Karolina stayed where she was, at the foot of the immense plaster replica of Nike of Samothrace, listening to their conversation with half an ear. Lars Franke, the art and design editor, made his way over to her.

"Hans tells me you want to step up your contribution," he said when they had said hi. "Fine by me. There's a Berthe Morisot exhibition in Copenhagen in a month or so—is that something you might be interested in?"

"I'm not sure... To be honest, I think Manet's portrait of her is much better than anything she painted herself."

Lars let out a brief, surprised bark of laughter. "But you write about images of women, and she portrays a female sphere."

"I'm afraid an upper-class woman's depiction of bourgeois family life isn't really my thing. I think you have more in common with her than I have."

She hadn't meant to sound abrasive, but she couldn't bring herself to apologize. Fortunately Lars seemed to think she was joking, and laughed again to cover his confusion.

"Will you at least think about it?" he said. "If you don't want to go, there will be plenty of other exhibitions to write about, but I like the idea of sending you off somewhere—you're a real expert. Then I can leave the kids to cover the galleries and the spring salon. I was in Paris myself last week; it's the Bonnard jubilee this year, so the Musée d'Orsay is staging a major exhibition of the Nabis group."

"Wow."

"It's a fantastic exhibition. Do you like them?"

"Absolutely, especially Vallotton. He's genuinely good."

Lars nodded and smiled at her.

"Genuinely good…" he repeated. "That's interesting. What else is genuinely good?"

She laughed. Was he flirting with her? Or did he really want to know what she thought? She pointed up at the figure of Nike.

"That, for example."

Lars nodded again.

"And that." She pointed to the plaster copy of the Laocoön Group a short distance away, Laocoön and his sons desperately trying to free themselves from the giant snakes that were coiling around their bodies and would soon kill them.

"I don't think many people would disagree with you."

"No, but do you know why they're good? They were produced during the Hellenistic period, which I think of as the Mannerism of ancient Greece. A kind of autumn for classical art. And they're good because they're pointing toward destruction. You can see something trembling within them, as if the marble is throbbing, writhing. It's impossible to regard this art in the same way with hindsight as contemporary society would have done, because when we look at it, we do so with the knowledge of history. We know these sculptures mark an epoch that is about to go under. That knowledge is like becoming aware of our own mortality; it changes our perspective completely. Nothing is innocent any longer. There can be no disinterested contemplation once we are aware of death."

"I think Kant might have something to say about that."

She shrugged. "An animal is capable of disinterested contemplation, a human being is not."

"But a human being can at least imagine the concept? You understand where I'm coming from?"

"Yes, but what's the point? Theory is totally meaningless if it can never be applied to reality."

Lars laughed again. "I'd really like you to write about Berthe Morisot. If you take that pessimistic view to Copenhagen, it will be a brilliant piece."

They went over to the bar for another glass of wine. Peter Sundman joined them and started talking about a proposal to build housing on an area of railroad track in central Stockholm; he was angry and wanted to write an article. Hans Jerup was standing at a bistro table a short distance away, eating dessert with a couple of literary critics. He really was very good-looking. So alive.

He noticed her glancing at him and beckoned her over. "Are you enjoying yourself?" he asked.

"Absolutely."

"Have you had dessert?"

She shook her head, and he pushed an untouched panna cotta across to her.

"There you go—it's delicious. I've already had two."

She tried it and nodded to show that she agreed with him.

"I enjoyed the other night," she said quietly.

"The thing is…" he said with his mouth close to her ear once more. "Tove's pregnant, so I have to behave myself now."

He winked at her, what kind of a wink was that? A wink that meant he would have liked to go back to her place anyway; he couldn't because of some kind of convention, but he still wanted to let her know that she was a woman with whom he wanted to cheat on his pregnant girlfriend?

Someone around the table asked him a question, he laughed and replied, she didn't hear a word. The panna cotta grew in her mouth, it wasn't delicious at all, it was unpleasantly heavy and creamy, there was a dull, fatty aftertaste, almost rancid, she forced herself to swallow before she left the table, made her way to the cloakroom through the cheerfully mingling correspondents, retrieved her jacket and went down the stairs, through the huddle of smokers outside. "Are you leaving already, Karolina?" someone called after her, she mumbled a yes, she had no idea who had spoken, she hurried out onto the sidewalk, out into the darkness.

He had gotten his beautiful girlfriend pregnant, of course he had. Because his girlfriend was the kind of woman you planned a future with. It wasn't fair.

What was the point of the feminist struggle, she thought as she passed Riddarhuset on the way to the Old Town, as long as the biology stayed the same? It would never be possible to do anything about the most basic injustice of all: the fact that the biologically superior female body was totally dependent on the continuation of life according to a fixed plan, on every woman meeting a man with whom she could reproduce within a preordained period of time.

Men were overrepresented at both the top and the bottom of society as a whole: there were more male geniuses and company directors, but also more underachievers, criminals and down-and-outs. From a purely biological point of view, the opposite was true: the female body, which at its zenith was both aesthetically perfect and so beautifully constructed that it could carry and bear a child, had a short best-before date. Half of a woman's life, maybe more, remained after the ability to reproduce had declined dramatically and then disappeared altogether, after the female body became biologically unfit for purpose. The male body, on the other hand, was unaffected by time in that respect. It was such a grotesque injustice, and it meant that a woman was forced to become a kind of disciplined project leader for her life, making sure she steered events in the right direction, taking command. Those women who failed became biological losers, while men could do whatever they wanted without taking responsibility for anything, yet still end up sitting there with the perfect nuclear family one day.

In the twenty-first century, in a culture that had put a lot of effort into denying biology, the most natural process appeared grotesque when it made its presence felt, especially at the social level where she now found herself, the urban middle class, where life was also about career and prestige and status, where self-realization and independence were key, and female biology was mainly an impractical relic of more primitive times. Maybe she had somehow believed that she had fooled the system when she devoted herself to study and research rather than building a family of her own, when she behaved in the same way as men had the privilege of doing, but perhaps it was the system that had fooled her. She had thought that if she didn't acknowledge it, she would simply be allowed to slip through; she had imagined that they had made an unspoken pact to ignore each other. Surely biology couldn't get the better of her, when she had read so many books?

Now everything she had achieved seemed utterly meaningless. Like diversionary tactics that hadn't worked.

The evening was dark and mild as she quickly walked toward Slussen through the Old Town, enveloped in a heavy, brooding feeling of nausea, as if it were a creature that had moved into her body and settled, intending to stay forever. It wouldn't be possible to get rid of it by vomiting, it wasn't that kind of nausea.

What if she tried to form a relationship with Robban in Gusum? She could probably plan her work schedule so that she could spend half her time over there, sit and write in his house. She might manage to get pregnant after a while. Have a baby who would grow up exactly as she had done, playing the same games of hide-and-seek and rounders, going on the same expeditions to the water tower and dilapidated summer cottages, the same lovely April twilights and mild summer evenings, the same sense of security. Her parents would be so pleased. Falling in love with Robban would be hard, maybe even impossible, but people had done worse things in order to achieve that nuclear family, she was sure of it. And he was kind, which was the best quality of all. She thought about the warmth in his voice when he said that she deserved a bit of luck, after she had told him about Anton and Ebba Ellis, even though he hadn't a clue what she was talking about.

And even if it's not possible to deserve things.

People lay sleeping in the pedestrian tunnels beneath Slussen, on pieces of cardboard or filthy mattresses, with their possessions in blue IKEA bags; it stank of dirt and bodies down there.

We don't deserve things. We might think we deserve a good grade or a promotion because we've worked hard, but in reality life is full of occasions when effort and input bear absolutely no relation to the dividend paid out. No one deserves to sleep on a piece of cardboard in a tunnel that stinks of piss, just as no one deserves love. Or the luck Robban had mentioned. Professional success—pure chance, because she happened to be mentoring a certain PhD candidate who turned out to be in possession of exceptionally interesting material. She certainly hadn't deserved or earned that success. No such compensatory mechanism exists in the universe.

The thought intensified the nausea, she had to stop by the wall on Katarinavägen, take deep breaths. She felt as if she was sitting on a carousel in the Gröna Lund amusement park, lurking in the darkness on the other side of the water, as if her entire stomach was being sucked downward.

We don't deserve things.

How stupid of her to regard the fact that Anton had been allocated to her as some kind of justice, to think that it would put things right, restore the balance in her life, compensate for everything that had gone wrong.

Life didn't work that way.

The more firmly her misgivings took root, the clearer the reality became: it was too good to be true.

What was it that had made her so happy? What did she actually know about Anton's project? She flicked through her brain like a card index, a series of images from a jerky old movie: Ebba Ellis, unknown female symbolist. Drawings featuring motifs taken from biblical stories and classical mythology, an element of surrealism, all very similar to the German symbolists. And Anton

Strömberg, PhD student with a background in the world of auction houses. He discovers Ebba Ellis, becomes fascinated by her work and decides to make her the subject of his dissertation. He receives a tip-off about the mysterious Lotte Baumann in Berlin, the owner of a series of letters between Ebba Ellis and Franz von Stuck—letters indicating that Ellis was the real originator behind some of von Stuck's best-known paintings, and that she constitutes a link to the German symbolist movement that has yet to be researched.

What a fantastic story it was, perfectly tailored to the contemporary insistence on achieving gender balance in the history of art.

And how fortunate for Anton that he had actually managed to find those letters. Otherwise he might have wasted an entire year living in Berlin on his postgraduate grant, enjoying the night life without having written a single line.

She hurried home, her heart pounding, she could almost hear it echoing in the stairwell as she waited for the old elevator to reach the ground floor.

She sat down at the computer and opened the Wikipedia page on Ebba Ellis once more. "Swedish artist, born 1864 in Kristianstad, died 1945 in Munich. Ellis studied art in Germany and Paris from 1882. She made her name primarily through her symbolist-influenced graphics."

There was a note at the bottom of the page stating that it was based on an article in the encyclopedia known as *Nordisk familjebok*. She followed the link to the issue of *Ord & Bild* containing Bertel Gripenberg's poem and Ebba Ellis's illustrations of Salome. The same pictures Anton had shown her in her office. Beyond that, there really was no more information about Ellis on the Internet. Every other match was irrelevant; most led to American ancestry research websites.

She tried to remember what Anton had told her. What was the name of the art dealer in Berlin who had put him in touch with Lotte Baumann? Dernberg? Dernburg? She googled her way to the conclusion that it must be Dernburg; there was an art store under that name on Kantstraße in Berlin. The web page was pale gray, sober and at the same time rather old-fashioned. A number of older graphics were pictured, but no prices were given. *"Anfrage per Email."*

She googled Lotte Baumann. There were women of that name, but none in Berlin. She found Facebook pages and LinkedIn profiles, but they were all young Lottes in different parts of Germany. None of the hits matched a Lotte Baumann who should be in her eighties now, and according to a German telephone directory, no Lotte Baumann was registered in Berlin. She tried Stuck + Baumann—no matches.

She couldn't think of anything else to google.

Restlessly she clicked on her university e-mail account and scrolled through the unread messages in her inbox. Anton had contacted her earlier that evening. "Text!" it said in the subject box. It was a brief, cheerful note: "Hi Karolina, thanks for the other day. I'm sending you the first chapters of my dissertation. See you soon! Anton"

She immediately opened the attached document. It consisted of just one chapter, plus a sloppy attempt at an introduction. The chapter focused on Ebba Ellis's work as an artist, and contained what looked like reasonable analyses of various pieces. The introduction was no more than an outline, and had presumably been written in haste, possibly that afternoon. None of it was particularly impressive. She tried to consider the text as she would have done if she hadn't known Anton at all. The fact that it was supposed to be the result of a year's work was simply unacceptable. She glanced through the introduction again; it was a high-flown account of Ellis's life and work, plus her contacts with von Stuck and the German symbolist movement. The style was careless, almost veering toward a dumbed-down approach.

"It's very clear that Ellis enjoyed both a high status and great influence in the contexts within which she moved. The spectacular exchange of letters recounts a series of events of considerable importance in the history of art. She writes about her first meeting with Stuck, which seems to have comprised an encounter at the restaurant Zum Löwen in Munich, where they initially had a furious argument—the cause is unknown—and then became friends for life. The letters also contain details of the origin of Stuck's most famous work, *Die Sünde*, and Ellis's critical role in that process. There are also many descriptions of the social life within artistic circles: New Year's 1902 is celebrated with a party in Stuck's studio, with Arnold Böcklin himself among the guests."

Karolina googled Zum Löwen in Munich; its website stated that it was a traditional German restaurant dating back to the 1870s. It was impossible to find any information about how Franz von Stuck had celebrated New Year's 1902, or what Böcklin might have been doing. Then she caught sight of the Wikipedia page on Böcklin, which was at the top of the list of hits. "... died 16 January 1901 at his home in San Domenico, Fiesole, Tuscany."

She leaned back, trying to understand the significance of what she had just read.

Maybe Anton had simply typed the date incorrectly. She went back to his introduction; there was a note accompanying the reference to the New Year's party. The note led her to a paragraph from a transcribed letter; the original was included in an appendix at the end of the document. In both the date was given as 1902.

Slowly she got to her feet and went over to one of the bookshelves, took out a catalogue from an exhibition of Böcklin's work that had been held in Stockholm in the nineties, opened it at the first page: "Arnold Böcklin (1827–1901)."

She didn't know whether she was trying to torture herself by looking it up in a book, or whether she thought it might prove something different. From a purely theoretical point of view, it could be that the year of Böcklin's death was incorrect all over the Internet. It had still been possible, during the few seconds it took her to walk over to the bookshelf and open the catalogue, that what was in the letter Anton claimed formed part of the correspondence between Stuck and Ebba Ellis was actually true. That the alleged date of Böcklin's death, 1901, was a silly mistake on Wikipedia which had then spread like an echo right across the Internet.

But of course that wasn't the case. The letters Anton quoted as his source, the basis for the whole of his groundbreaking dissertation, simply didn't match the reality.

She spent a little while longer googling the details she was able to make out from the barely legible letters in the appendix. In one of them Stuck was mentioned as "von Stuck" in 1904, when in fact he didn't add "von" until 1906, when he was awarded the Order of Merit of the Bavarian Crown for his work. The date of his painting of a centaur and a blonde nymph was also incorrect; she checked and double-checked then checked again, both in her books and in every source she could find on the Internet. It was still wrong.

It was sloppy, even if these were only minor points in a solid narrative, created by a person who was exactly like his lie: dedicated but negligent, gifted but lazy. No doubt he had had a very enjoyable year in Berlin.

The idea enraged her; she felt like grabbing her phone and sending him a text, telling him that he had been exposed, it was all over. That she wanted to know exactly what he had lied about, every single detail, just as a wife whose husband has cheated on her needs to know exactly what he has done, masochistically wallowing in her own gullibility and unsuspecting nature. She wanted to call him, scream at him, demand to know what he thought she was going to do now, how he could have been so fucking dumb. She could hear herself, torn between hating him and pleading with him, her voice full of self-pity as she asked how he could do this to her. "Don't you understand that I have nothing now?" she wanted to yell, and the realization that this was absolutely true filled her with nausea once more; she could hear Lennart Olsson's voice in her head: "The history of art is a compost heap, particularly when it comes to women. The only thing we can do is start digging. Sometimes we find something valuable, but unfortunately the rest of the time there's nothing but dung."

But the most repulsive aspect of it all was the fact that what there had been between her and Anton, which she had experienced as a powerful attraction, a feeling of deep mutual understanding, something that was above all honest, had also been false on his part. Part of a plan, a way to bind her closer, make her more loyal, more uncritical.

How could she have believed that someone like him would want her? How stupid had she been?

Her head was spinning, she had to go and lie down. How could everything go so wrong for her? How could she be so ill-suited to life, so inadequate?

She closed her eyes, thought about cold and ice, fresh air, to try to fight off the sickness. The polar bear in the ad for throat lozenges. The Antarctic. Svalbard. There was a gigantic seed bank in Svalbard, like a Noah's ark for plants from all over the world. She had seen pictures of it: a concrete box, like a strong room the same shape as an old hard drive, built into the mountain. The location had been chosen because of the permafrost, which would guarantee the optimum temperature for the seeds, giving them long-term stability. No earthquakes would shake the bank, the rising water levels caused by climate change would never reach it. Humanity could destroy everything that grows, then fetch the seeds to cultivate crops once more, forests could be raised anew, flowers tempted back to the surface of the earth.

Certain flowers created their own seed bank, which was a fascinating thought. The seeds of *Geranium lanuginosum* can grow only after a forest fire; they lie dormant in the ground, and are activated by the heat when a blaze rages through the trees. It is not known how long they can wait, but viable seeds have been found in places where there hasn't been a fire for several hundred years.

It was so well organized that it was hard not to have faith in a god; she often felt that way when she thought about nature. Everything was calibrated to such a degree of perfection that it was almost impossible to believe that someone hadn't planned it all, that it wasn't the result of meticulous and extensive calculations.

But time was the god. Those timescales so dizzyingly vast that she was incapable of understanding them: they had fine-tuned nature into a single, immense and smoothly functioning system where everything had its place in a greater order, everything had a function, everything ate and was eaten, working together, forming a chain. This system had been shaped over an unimaginable period of time, tested during the course of millions of years. Anything that didn't work went under, was kicked out. The day forest fires no longer happened, for some reason, *Geranium lanuginosum* would die out, as almost all species had done before it. Of the life that once existed on our planet, 99.9 percent is extinct. Species that were poorly adapted to the circumstances in which they lived were slowly wound down, went under, were forgotten.

Lock me away in the seed bank in Svalbard, she thought. And don't let me out until I can cope with living a normal life.

October was usually her favorite month, but this year she hardly noticed it. She felt apathetic as she waited for the number two bus at Ersta Hospital in the morning, got off at Slussen and changed to the red line on the subway, tried to find a block of empty seats so that she could be alone. She had realized that the subway was populated only by crazies between the morning and evening rush hours, crazies and retirees and those on parental leave.

A man with a shaven head, wearing a military green anorak, came and sat down opposite her. On his knee was a book in a library binding, from which he was energetically making notes on the back of a receipt in microscopic handwriting. The piece of paper was almost full of his tiny, firm letters; she was sure he had no intention of leaving even a fraction of an inch empty. He looked hard, as she imagined men who had fought in a war must look: a determined expression, a tense jawline, something haggard about his features, revealing the fact that this was a man who had probably killed people. In addition, there was something sadistic about his whole appearance, as if he hadn't hurt others only because he was forced to do so, but because he had enjoyed it. Maybe he was some kind of sexual sadist. She wondered what it would be like to go to bed with somebody like him. What would he do to her? Tie her up? Hit her, spank her? She remembered the advice columns' well-meaning exhortations, pointing out that safety and trust were key if you were curious about that type of sex, it wouldn't be like that with somebody like him. He looked totally unreliable.

Just as the train began to slow down on its approach to the station by the university, he raised his head and stared straight at her. His eyes were so piercing that for a second she thought he knew what she was thinking, and that the way he was looking at her was an acceptance, a reply to an invitation she hadn't even issued. She was overcome with embarrassment; she got up quickly and hurried toward the nearest door.

Later she found herself sitting in a meeting where Lennart Olsson was talking about an interdisciplinary research project on the state of exile, which he was very enthusiastic about. He felt he was ideally suited to participate, because several of the artists in his field had been in exile: the Jewess Elsa Wolff, for example, who had moved in the circle around the movement known as Die Brücke when she was young. She had fled to Stockholm at the outbreak of the Second World War, and had lived and worked in Gröndal, where she had married a customs official. It was an unwritten story that deserved to be told, just as her art deserved a decent re-evaluation both from a historical and a market point of view. Karolina listened with half an ear, wondering in passing how many pieces by Elsa Wolff Lennart owned. She looked down when he asked for opinions, she didn't care about the state of exile today, she didn't really understand what the project was about.

It was as if her brain consisted of two separate chambers. One was brooding on the fact that she was a failure. Why had she opted for an academic career? Why hadn't she settled for less? Stayed in Östergötland, trained for something ordinary, a teacher, social worker, something that would have provided her with permanent employment, security, enough money to live reasonably well; she could have met a nice, ordinary man during her training, they could have moved in together, gotten married, had two kids, gone on vacation maybe twice a year, eventually bought a summer cottage, possibly in northern Småland where property was still cheap, it would be close to her parents, weekends would have meant spending time with the family rather than working, and above all weekends wouldn't have meant being alone.

What had actually made her happy about the life she had made for herself? Self-realization might seem desirable in comparison to its opposite, but as the only alternative it wasn't especially attractive. Suddenly it seemed as if the nameplate on her door was mocking her, that "Karolina Andersson, Professor of Art" was nothing more than a sad indictment. That was her life, summarized in just a few words. A life should contain more than there is space for on a nameplate.

And even those words would lose value if it became known that she had let herself be fooled by a PhD candidate, she thought that evening as she stood at the stove stirring a pan of tomato sauce. The other part of her brain had taken over; it had no time for self-pity, but twisted and turned the situation like a Rubik's Cube, trying to be rational. She could report Anton to the disciplinary board, that was probably what she ought to do with a candidate who had tried to cheat in his dissertation in order to divert attention from his own lack of effort, but that would inevitably rebound on her. Why hadn't she kept a closer eye on things during the first year, when there had been virtually no sign of life from Anton during his time in Berlin? And how could she possibly have believed his stories? It would be extremely embarrassing if someone were to suggest that she had been easy to deceive because Anton was so charming and good-looking. She pictured the meaningful glances in the lunchroom, the raised eyebrows; she could hear the gossip, the subdued sniggering in the corridors, the hints about a romance. No one knew for sure, but they all found it very easy to imagine there was something going on.

The tomato sauce didn't turn out well, in spite of the fact that she left it to simmer for a long time. It had an unpleasant metallic taste; she added both salt and sugar to try to rectify it, but to no avail. Then she overcooked the pasta. It was a miserable dinner.

The worst of it was that she wouldn't even be able to get angry when they laughed at her in the corridors, she thought as she ate; she would think she deserved it. Because she had been so gullible. It had been easy for him to work out that she would be delighted with his tale, just as delighted as he had been with the exchange of letters he had allegedly discovered. Perhaps even more delighted. He hadn't even had to make much of an effort; she had fooled herself. She had reveled in the lie as if she were starving. As if she were desperate.

No one could have wanted the story Anton had served up more than Karolina; he must have been so happy when he realized that.

She stopped with her fork halfway to her mouth.

There might be one person who would be equally excited.

She tried to imagine how Lennart Olsson would react if he were offered Anton's story; it wasn't hard. The thought of Ebba Ellis's relative and his extensive collection of her work would immediately set Lennart wondering about the possibility of acquiring a number of etchings and paintings for himself, before setting in motion the machinery to increase their value, while at the same time giving his own career an even greater luster. He would be spellbound by Anton's account of his dealings in Berlin, possibly presented in an even more appealing form; he would examine the alleged correspondence between Franz von Stuck and Ebba Ellis with uncritical eyes, his mind filled with dreams of money and success. Elsa Wolff, the forgotten artist of whom he had spoken with such enthusiasm at the meeting, was nothing compared to this.

She tried to calm her mind, poured herself a glass of cold white wine, sank down on the sofa and switched on the TV at random. The latest news was about to begin on TV4. She had almost stopped watching television following the split with Karl Johan, who had been obsessed with never missing a bulletin, as far as possible; she had hated it, and had done her best to avoid the news out of sheer spite ever since. When the headlines were announced she remembered another reason why she didn't like these programs: they were far too depressing. There had been a terrorist attack in North Africa, a number of people—it wasn't clear how many, probably at least fifty—had been taken hostage at an international tourist hotel. A doctor in the south of Sweden was suspected of having sexually abused a series of children. And there had been an earthquake in Southeast Asia, which fortunately had caused only moderate damage. A tsunami could have cost tens of thousands of lives, a reporter explained over an erratic telephone connection. The camera flew over densely populated areas close to the sea, and it wasn't difficult to imagine the disastrous consequences of a tidal wave.

It was so dreadful to think that nothing in life was predictable. Maybe it was a measure of a person's viability, how well they adapted to rapidly changing circumstances over and over again without breaking down or going crazy. She thought back to something she had read recently about the catastrophe that had struck Lisbon in 1775: it was November 1, and the feast of All Saints' Day was being celebrated in one of the world's most important cities in terms of trade. At nine thirty in the morning, when most people were in church, the ground began to shake. Soon huge fissures opened up in streets and squares, buildings crashed to the ground with a deafening roar, and the sky grew dark with a Stygian fog.

In the main port of that great seafaring nation, a splendid quayside made entirely of marble had been constructed, solid and beautiful. A number of large ships were moored there, and the citizens of Lisbon fled to the open area surrounding the docks in order to avoid the collapsing buildings. They thought they were safe there.

The harbor was crowded with people when the tsunami struck. The water rose and swept in across the city, the tidal wave was carried on into the country along the river Tagus, then it drew back with such powerful suction that the entire riverbed was left dry. In the harbor itself, the waters swallowed everything—ships, people, the splendid marble quay.

Those who survived both the earthquake and the tsunami might have thought it was all over. Perhaps they had begun to consider what was left of their homes, if and when they might be able to return to them. Perhaps they had begun to wonder tentatively what the immediate future would look like. Then came the fire. Anything in the city that had not been destroyed by the earthquake or the water was consumed in an inferno that raged for six days.

New plans had to be made. They had to start all over again, from nothing. The people of Portugal started this new chapter in their lives by blaming one another, just as contemporary society does after disasters and accidents and terrorist atrocities. Where did the blame lie? It was a punishment from God, most were in agreement on that point, but for what? Who had brought it upon their country? Protestants, Catholics and Jesuits were all convinced that the fault lay with the others.

That was one advantage of having a god, Karolina thought; it made life more manageable even at the worst of times. However unfathomable the ways of God might seem, we can rest safe in the knowledge that nothing happens without a purpose.

In the absence of a god, we have to try to make life manageable on our own terms.

She got up from the sofa, sat down at the computer and opened up her university e-mail account. All at once her mind was calm and clear. She clicked on "compose" and addressed the message to both Lennart and Anton. Would it be possible for the three of them to meet up this week? It wouldn't take long, but it was urgent.

.   .   .

She rarely cried these days. When she was young she had wept over everything, and enjoyed it. During one period in her teenage years she had exposed herself to the saddest books and movies, over and over again, seeing her tears as proof that she was an unusually sensitive person. With hindsight she despised the fact that she had let herself be moved by such sentimental nonsense; behavior like that was something you could indulge in before you had real problems.

She hadn't cried when she left Karl Johan. He had stayed in the apartment and bought her out, which was insane from a financial point of view, because it was an attractive property, and would no doubt have sold for far more than she got from him if there had been a bidding war. But it was a practical arrangement, she couldn't face any hassle or setbacks, she had a guilty conscience, and she just wanted to get out of there.

She hadn't cried when the movers arrived, when she walked around pointing out the pieces of furniture they were to take, when she broke up the home she and Karl Johan had built together over many years. She hadn't cried in the new apartment, although it had been a close thing when she stood in her living room among the unopened boxes, with the furniture all over the place. At the time she had thought she had nothing; how stupid could she be? What did she know about having nothing? That was only six months ago.

Sometimes it seemed to her that she had postponed the real tears whenever she had had a reason to cry. That she still hadn't cleared away the remains of her breakup with Karl Johan, or her disappointment over Anders—on both occasions. That the real tears still lay deep inside her, like a swab left behind in the body after an operation. One day they would make their presence felt, and she wouldn't be able to stop crying, they would break through every barricade with the violence of a dam bursting.

But that day would have to wait.

At the moment the sense of having regained control of the situation brought an enjoyable serenity. She almost thought there was an air of superiority about her when she glanced in the hall mirror before leaving home; she looked dignified. Outside, the October air was pleasant. What a wonderful time of year it was. Even the turquoise buildings on the university campus shimmered in the autumn sun like jewels, a city of precious stones. All at once she found them beautiful; there was something promising in that shimmer. A promise for the future.

As she was pouring herself a coffee in the lunchroom, Peter Tallfalk came in with an empty mug in his hand; he smiled as soon as he saw her.

"Karolina—good to see you. I have something for you."

"Oh?"

The coffee machine was humming loudly, there was something secretive about his smile now. When his mug was full, he tilted his head to indicate that she should come with him.

His office was cluttered with books. Karolina had heard that some of their more tidy-minded colleagues had complained about the fact that merely walking past the door and having to see all those piles of books was upsetting for them. Personally she thought it looked cozy. There was a framed exhibition poster on the wall, "The Age of Dürer and Holbein," and a dusty Kentia palm in a pot in one corner gave the place a kind of nineteenth-century air.

Peter sat down at the desk and handed her a stiff envelope.

"What's this?"

"Open it and see."

The envelope was full of small pieces of paper. She took one out; it was creamy white, with a picture of a woman in a garden printed on it. It was a back view, and she was reaching up to a lilac bush in full bloom. The drawing was done in Jugendstil, with strong, flowing lines. Beneath the image were the words "Ex libris Karolina Andersson."

"What's this?" she said again.

Peter was beaming at her. "You can see what it is."

"You've made a set of bookplates? For me?"

"Well, I didn't make them personally . . . but yes, they're for you."

She stared at the little picture of the woman and the lilac as her eyes filled with tears and everything became blurred.

"Oh, Peter," she said in a small voice. "That's lovely."

He looked pleased and slightly worried at the same time; maybe he was afraid she was going to go to pieces in front of him.

"They won't last very long," he said, possibly to avoid an embarrassing silence, "there are only a hundred. But you can order more. And remember the paper is sensitive to acids, so be careful which glue you use. The best thing is to make a paste yourself from flour and water."

She leaned forward and gave him a hug, an awkward, uncomfortable hug because he was sitting down and she was standing.

"Thank you," she said with her mouth close to his ear. He patted her back awkwardly as if to say "You're welcome."

She would invite him to dinner, she thought as she walked back to her office. Leyla too, so that there would be no misunderstanding. She was no master chef, but she could produce a perfectly decent meal if she wanted to; she was capable of cooking other things apart from tomato sauce. She just hadn't had any reason to do so for a long time.

As she pushed the envelope into her bag she could see herself mixing flour and water in a bowl, then sitting down at the kitchen table to stick the plates into her books. She would start this evening. A small brush would probably be useful, she must get one. She glanced at the clock on the wall. Almost eleven.

Lennart Olsson was exactly on time; he walked in and greeted her in a way that was unusually subdued. He was probably wondering what she wanted. He sat down in the visitor's chair and started talking about a symposium on psychoanalysis that the journal *Notos* was planning in connection with a future issue; he had agreed to take part. Apparently several of the female artists in his field of research had been very interested in psychoanalysis.

Shortly after eleven Anton swept in, looking very cheerful. As if he were expecting a meeting that would somehow be to his advantage. No doubt that was his general approach to life, Karolina thought. He was used to getting what he wanted in every situation. He pulled up a wooden chair from the corner of her room and sat down next to Lennart. Both men looked at her with curiosity. She cleared her throat.

"I'm sure you're wondering what this is all about," she began. "I don't want to make a big thing of it, so I'll get straight to the point: I just don't think I'm the right person to continue as Anton's supervisor."

She paused to let the news sink in. Anton's eyes were darting all over the place, while Lennart's expression was full of anticipation, as if he thought he knew where she was going with this, and was desperately hoping not to be disappointed.

"And to be honest, Lennart..." she went on, turning to face him, "I think you'll do a far better job than I would on this project. It's obvious to all of us that the basis of Anton's research is something unique, which must be curated in the best possible way. The day this is made public it will attract a huge amount of attention, and you have far more experience than I do when it comes to dealing with that kind of thing. Your book on the female modernists also means you have a wider network of contacts than I do."

She couldn't tell whether she sounded convincing, but it didn't seem to matter. The two men on the other side of the desk were ready to believe her: Anton because he was terrified of being exposed, Lennart because he simply thought he was being rewarded with something he deserved.

She caught Anton's eye for a second; she could see that in spite of the fact that he had lived with the risk of being caught out for a long time, this was a shock. He hadn't expected her to hand him over to someone else. Maybe he had felt more sure of himself after their night together, thinking that he had bound her to him more intimately than he could have dared to hope for. She could also see the unease in his eyes, the worry that she had seen through him and now had a hold over him, and that Lennart might not be quite so easy to dupe.

That was exactly what she wanted him to think, but it would be a long time before Lennart started to question anything in Anton's dissertation, she was sure of it. Because unlike Karolina, Lennart thought he deserved the acclaim this breakthrough would bring.

In the best-case scenario they would get as far as Anton's disputation before Lennart realized that the letters referred to in the dissertation were nothing more than a sloppily executed collection of fakes. A sharp-eyed opponent, who had nothing to gain from the story of Ebba Ellis and Franz von Stuck, would have no difficulty in spotting the cracks. And once those cracks began to spread, the whole thing would collapse in no time, leaving nothing but the work of a forgotten female artist among many. An interesting artist, admittedly, but not one who was likely to generate renown and international accolades.

Lennart was looking at her as if he felt that justice had been done. Fantastic. Karolina thought so too.

He sat up a little straighter.

"Of course I'll take over," he said in an authoritative tone of voice. "You seem to have had a lot on your plate recently, Karolina. It's probably a good idea to let something go."

What did he mean, a lot on her plate recently? She had probably never had less to do than she had this fall. Was it his way of telling her she looked exhausted? Couldn't he say a single word without provoking her? She had to bite her tongue to stop herself from snapping back at him; instead she forced herself to smile.

"Thank you, Lennart," she murmured. Then she turned to Anton. "I hope this is okay by you?"

Her tone made it clear that this wasn't really a question, that she was assuming he wouldn't complain. He looked both angry and troubled; there was no doubt that the new arrangement was far from okay. However, he knew he couldn't object. He stared at her, his expression dark. She stared right back.

I don't want anything more to do with you, her eyes told him. You only have yourself to blame.

What do you actually know? he asked her silently.

Enough to realize you're lying.

I'll report you, he said.

In that case I'll report you.

When he understood that anger was getting him nowhere, he tried pleading with her instead. His expression was suddenly warm, tender even, just as when they had sat close together on her sofa. She could almost hear him saying her name, just as he had said it that night, over and over again. She had liked her name when he said it.

Don't do this, he said. Think about us.

She had to make an effort not to laugh out loud, a dry, joyless little laugh that bubbled up inside her when she looked at him. She didn't know if it was the laugh of a winner or a loser.

Do you think I don't know that it was all lies? she asked him. Do you think I don't know that it was part of your plan?

You're wrong, he said.

She caught herself shaking her head. Maybe he was being honest, it was impossible to tell. Maybe taking her home and going to bed with her hadn't been part of his plan, maybe he too had been captivated by the spark between them, by how well they got on, maybe he had found her attractive and interesting. Or maybe she was just flattering herself. It no longer mattered anyway; sitting here opposite him, she felt absolutely nothing for him. There was nothing charming about his ill-fitting jacket and unkempt appearance. She saw a liar. A good liar, better than her, she had to give him that. He and Lennart would make a good team. She felt like a marriage broker who had just matched a couple who would be very happy together, as long as Lennart didn't suspect that he had been deceived right from the start. At the moment he couldn't imagine such a thing; he was beaming with delight.

"I have to admit I'm very curious about your material, Anton," he said enthusiastically.

Anton met Karolina's eye for a second; he suddenly looked afraid. She had never seen him afraid before, and she had had no idea how satisfying it would be.

Lennart was still talking; asking about the circumstances surrounding the discovery of the letters, then about one or two details relating to content before suggesting that this pleasant meeting should perhaps continue over lunch at the Faculty Club. He had a permanent booking there every Tuesday and Thursday. Karolina quickly made her excuses; it was obvious that Anton would have liked to do the same, but Lennart persuaded him before he had the chance to open his mouth—the fish was excellent, he said as he got to his feet, nodding to Anton to follow suit, it was never as dry and uninspiring as it could be in some places, it was well worth the extra money it cost to dine there rather than picking up a sandwich or a salad in one of the cafes on campus. Karolina heard his babbling slowly die away down the corridor as the two of them disappeared.

She waited a few minutes before leaving. She walked along the corridor, down the stairs and out of the building, past the parking lot and the bus stops, and turned onto the path leading to the Natural History Museum. The sky was clear, the impressive poplars between the university and the museum towering above her in their autumn attire like tall yellow flames against the blue background.

Perhaps this was her forest fire, she thought. All through the fall, one long, low-intensity baptism of fire. But it wouldn't break her, even if it had felt that way while it was going on. She would emerge from this ready for something new, just like *Geranium lanuginosum*.

She stopped in the vast open space in front of the museum and stood directly below the entrance, gazing up at the huge building. It really did look like a body, she could see that now, with the cupola as a head in the middle. It reminded her of the mosaic on the wall in the community center in Gusum, where she had gone to Sunday school and confirmation classes, eaten cake and drunk coffee after the christenings and funerals she had managed to attend before she moved away: a stylized 1970s version of Jesus, holding out his arms to embrace those who wanted to come to him.

Her body felt light as she began to climb the steps. Light and clean.

How had Gavriila felt when the experiment was suddenly broken off? How had she found out that it was all over?

Had someone told her in the morning, after she had washed and dressed in her little room, then gone down to the kitchen for breakfast? The atmosphere had been subdued, one or two people looked as if they'd been crying. A row of pale faces, one of the lab assistants, his expression grave, had informed her that Dr. Ivanov was dead.

Gavriila didn't really know the doctor all that well. She knew virtually nothing about him as a person, or his private life. He hadn't mentioned a family to her, apart from his son Ilya Ivanov Junior, who still worked at the research station but seemed less and less interested in his father's experiments.

She and Ivanov had spoken almost exclusively about experiments and about banal, everyday matters: the weather, the food that was served at the station, the cat that had started hanging around by the main door and had now moved into the ground floor, where it was regularly fed by the staff. They were both delighted by this. She had felt as if there was a special bond between her and Ivanov, along with a quiet, warm humor that contributed to the strong sense of intimacy she had experienced with him. He had been kind to her. In return she had been prepared to place her life in his hands, knowing that he would look after this gift in the best possible way. It was a matter of complete trust, of the kind she could vaguely remember feeling toward the adults who had been close to her when she was a child. It was such a long time since she had felt utterly safe with another person. And now it was over.

Her eyes had filled with tears, she had tried to blink them away. The research station wasn't a place for an emotional outburst. It was a place for self-control and restraint.

"What does this mean?" she had asked in a small voice.

"It means we're finished," the lab assistant had replied. "You can go home."

"But this is the only home I have."

The lab assistant had shaken his head. "In that case you'll have to get yourself a new one. This project has been canceled with immediate effect."

It must have been such a shock to discover that the thing she had thought of as giving her existence its only goal and purpose over the past year no longer existed. That every single aspect of her life was going to have to change again. And that she had no idea how that was going to happen.

Karolina pictured Gavriila slowly getting up from the breakfast table, going outside, walking the streets of Sukhumi down to the shore. It was March 21, 1932, a mild early spring day, almost fifteen degrees Celsius, the town enveloped in a gray, shimmering, mother-of-pearl mist. Grubby, flaking facades, palm trees, the roar of traffic on the streets, everyday life continuing. Everyday life continuing without her.

The shore is deserted. It is Monday, people with ordinary lives have other things to do at this time of day. Gavriila cannot see the horizon, it is too misty. It is like standing in an enormous gray room, in an emptiness so palpable that she can feel it physically, she is literally nothing there on the shore, she dissolves, becomes one with the mist in the air. She closes her eyes. It is like the state we are in just before we fall asleep, when first our body, then our consciousness slowly grows numb. Perhaps this is what it feels like to die.

No.

She opens her eyes.

No one else is going to die today.

Even if she can't see them right now, she thinks, there are things waiting for her behind the gray curtain. She doesn't quite know what they are, and at the moment it is impossible to hazard a guess, but the mist will disperse. She will be paid for the experiment; it is not a large sum, but it is more money than she has ever had before, and she will be able to start afresh. First of all she must find somewhere to live, then she will get a job. The rest will follow.

Her whole body suddenly feels light, and somehow secure. How can she feel secure now? She has no idea; it is a new sensation.

The herring gulls are screaming, high in the sky the sun is beginning to break through, she turns her face up toward it.

It is spring, she thinks. Life goes on.

THERESE BOHMAN is a columnist for *Expressen*, writing about literature, art, culture, and fashion. Her debut novel, *Drowned*, was published by Other Press in 2012, followed by *The Other Woman* in 2016. She lives in Sweden.

MARLAINE DELARGY has translated novels by John Ajvide Lindqvist, Kristina Ohlsson, and Helene Tursten, as well as *A Fortune Foretold* by Agneta Pleijel and Henning Mankell's *After the Fire*. She serves on the editorial board of the *Swedish Book Review*. She lives in England.

▐▌ OTHER PRESS

Also by Therese Bohman

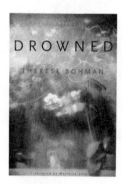

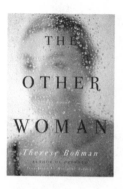

DROWNED

Mixing hothouse sensuality with ice-cold fear on every page, this thriller delves deep into the feminine soul and exposes the continuing oppression of women in Sweden's presumed egalitarian society.

"Author Therese Bohman could be lumped in with the other Scandinavian authors who have taken over the mystery world since *The Girl with the Dragon Tattoo*, but her story is more quiet and nuanced, her writing lush enough to create a landscape painting with every scene. No shoot-outs, showdowns, or explosions end this story, but be prepared to gasp all the same, not with fear, but with understanding." —*O, The Oprah Magazine*

THE OTHER WOMAN

A psychological novel where questions of class, status, and ambition loom over a young woman's passionate love affair.

"Erotic and shrewd... [Therese Bohman's] prose is breathtaking... An elegant, rich take on an age-old narrative." —*Publishers Weekly*

"Philosophical, passionate, and pensive — a novel that explores the psychology of both intimacy and lust." —*Kirkus Reviews*

"This captivating, character-driven tell-all provides the reader with a unique insight... And [Bohman's] bashfully charming leading lady keeps you hooked until the very last page." —*New York Daily News*

You might also be interested in:

QUICKSAND
by **Malin Persson Giolito**

NAMED A BEST BOOK OF 2017 BY NPR

NAMED BEST SWEDISH CRIME NOVEL OF THE YEAR BY THE SWEDISH CRIME WRITERS ACADEMY

An incisive courtroom thriller that raises questions about the nature of love, the disastrous side effects of guilt, and the function of justice.

"A remarkable new novel...Giolito writes with exceptional skill. She keeps us guessing a long time and the outcome, when it arrives, is just as it should be." —*Washington Post*

"Giolito's astonishing English-language debut is a dark exploration of the crumbling European social order and the psyche of rich Swedish teens...Masterful." —*Booklist* (starred review)

WILLFUL DISREGARD
by **Lena Andersson**

WINNER OF THE AUGUST PRIZE

A novel about a perfectly reasonable woman's descent into the delusions of unrequited love. Bitingly funny and darkly fascinating, *Willful Disregard* is a story about how willingly we betray ourselves in the pursuit of love.

"Gripped me like an airport read... perfect." —Lena Dunham

"Alas, most women have lived this story. Though few will have told it so well. Compelling and keenly observant." —Lionel Shriver, author of *We Need to Talk About Kevin*

"A story of the heart written with bracing intellectual rigor. It is a stunner, pure and simple." —Alice Sebold, best-selling author of *The Lovely Bones* and *Lucky*